THE TURNING
OF THE WHEEL

The Turning of the Wheel
The Assassins of Harmony: Book One
Copyright © 2022 by Jamie McNabb
All rights reserved

Cover design by Allyson Longueira
Map design by Brandon Swann
Cover art copyright © Roberto Atzeni | Dreamstime.com

Ebook ISBN: 978-1-948447-13-3
Trade Paperback ISBN: 978-1-948447-25-6

Published by Soapbox Rising Press

THE TURNING OF THE WHEEL

THE ASSASSINS OF HARMONY: BOOK ONE

JAMIE MCNABB

SOAPBOX RISING PRESS

THE METROPOLITANATE OF THE INLAND EMPIRE AND THE HOLY OREGON

Lower Columbia River

The Metropolitanate of The Inland Empire and The Holy Oregon

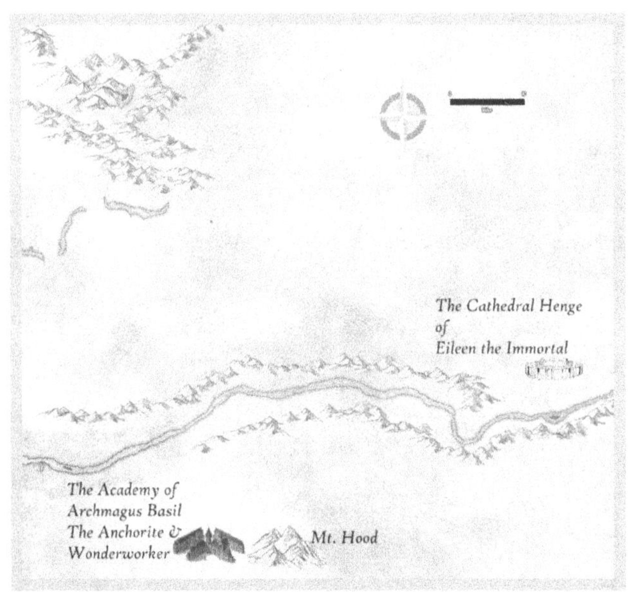

Upper Columbia River

ONE

When the hour of execution arrived, Edmund, the chieftain of Clan Iredale, stood at the head of his family. Included in the group was the condemned man's son, Vlod.

It was a defiant move, that choice to include the son of a heretic, but Edmund could do no less. He had ought to have done much more.

They had arrayed themselves on the chieftain's balcony, which overlooked the inner ward of Olney Castle.

They were on their home ground, at least. Olney was the Iredale's seat of government, Edmund's principal residence, and his ultimate stronghold.

Being there helped to soothe the agony but it also redoubled the peril. It signaled their weakness and the Mother Metropolitan's overarching power.

A child of nine, Vlod stood in plain view. It was raining. The rain was cold and sharp-edged, a slashing drizzle, but the boy made no effort to shield himself. Rather, he held his head up, enabling the near sleet to sting his face.

From cloak to boots, Edmund had dressed Vlod in grays and browns and blacks, the somber hues, but the clothes were the finest possible, the attire of a chieftain's favored son.

Thus, the warning stood clear, as inescapable as the rain, as inescapable as the Mother Metropolitan's will.

The storm had begun as a splotch of low pressure out in the Gulf of Alaska. The low had deepened, and as it had done so, its temperament had changed. No longer content to play, it had become a winter storm, a true child of January, of the God Janus, two-faced and ever-changing.

The storm had doubled and redoubled. Its winds had pushed the waves higher and higher, smashing over the crests, transforming them into avalanches of foam, and streaking them out to leeward.

When the storm had gathered sufficient strength, when it had grown restless, it had closed ranks and had marched off to the southeast.

A week later, it had swaggered ashore across a front hundreds of kilometers wide. Its center could have landed on the west coast of Vancouver Island, or at Grays Harbor, or at Yaquina Bay, or at Coos Bay, but it hadn't. Rather than striking any of those places, its center had hit the mouth of the Columbia River. It had hit like a drunk hoping to start a brawl.

For several hours the wind and the rain had flown at Olney's battlements, and it had howled through the streets of Fort George, the Iredale's capitol and the port city that had grown up, century by century, between the castle and the riverbank.

But then, with the arrival from upriver of the execution party, the storm had obediently lain down, as though the Mother Metropolitan's authority had also given her command of the weather. The wind had lessened, and the rain had ameliorated to a cold, penetrating drizzle. The storm had transformed itself into a smug assassin.

The shift had surprised no one. The storms of the northern Pacific are nothing if not fickle creatures, especially along this stretch of coast, this run of sand and rock and rivers and trees, watched over by Olney Castle.

Down in the inner ward, Vlod's father, Shivananda, was about to be burned at the stake for heresy. The wood, the pitch, and the torches were already in place, and Vlod's father had already been chained to the stake.

The rain glistened on the paving stones and on the stake and on the chains and on the man's face. The face was impassive, an utter blank, but it was as pale as though it belonged to a corpse. His left eye was swollen shut, and blood was streaming down from the left corner of his mouth. Mixed with saliva, it hung in long, dripping strings.

Edmund had forbidden his daughters, Dagna and Brenna, aged five and seven, from attending, but equally he couldn't have prevented his son, Morven, now twelve, from watching, from delighting in the spectacle.

From gloating?

That possibility sickened Edmund, but he forced his mind away. The child was young, his excitement natural.

Morven darted this way and that, hoping to find a better place from which to watch.

Annoria, Edmund's wife, sunk her fingers into Morven's shoulder, arched an eyebrow, and with no wasted words, convinced him to stand at her side. He was to be quiet, unmoving, impassive. To give nothing away. Not one thing. He was to wipe that snotty smile from his face. If she so much as glimpsed it again, he'd be the sorrier for it.

Vlod stood between his chieftain and the clan's battlemaster, Wolfram. Wolfram was Edmund's younger brother and the overall commander of the Iredale's military forces.

Wolfram was a large man. He was a full head taller than Edmund, and he was broader through the shoulders. A lifelong warrior, he was the sort of fighter who would rather attack across an open field than defend from behind a stone wall.

When the liquor was flowing, many said that it was Wolfram who ought to have acceded to the chieftaincy, not Edmund. They said that it was Wolfram who was the better man, the better strategist and the superior tactician.

Alas, they observed, while reaching for the bottle yet again, he had been born too late. He was out of his proper order by a piddling two years.

Had Edmund and Wolfram been born the other way around, they whispered, had the Gods and the Generations chosen differently, it would have changed everything.

But that was the way it was with the Gods and the Generations, those mongers of fate: the Goddess, Her pantheon, and the Generations, the holy ancestors of humanity. They chose as they saw fit. One could question, one could complain, one could bargain, one could thrash around, but in the end, obedience was unavoidable.

Even the demons and the devils obeyed, so what hope did human beings have to go their own individual ways?

Edmund and Wolfram smelled of well-worn leather and fresh tobacco smoke, of the new oil on their swords and daggers, of damp wool, and of the traces of mud on their boots.

It was midmorning, and rain was doing nothing to lessen the stench in the inner ward. That stench was a mixture of odors from the boiling pitch and the smoking torches. The air also smelled of wet basalt, wet roofing tiles, wet horses, and wet men-at-arms.

They were the Mother Metropolitan's men-at-arms, formed up in their rigid ranks and files, neatly squared.

Olney's inner ward smelled of the rain itself, too, January-cold and salt-laden.

Ocean rain.

Vlod's father loved that smell, and he exulted in the feel of that type of rain.

Vlod wondered if his father, chained to the stake, could smell the rain, that special rain, fresh in from the Pacific. Vlod hoped that he could.

Vlod listened to the charges, the verdict, and the sentence of death by burning.

He caught the eager rustling of the torches.

His father stood on top of a log pyre, chain-bound to a heavy timber post, the stake.

The Mother Metropolitan's people had stacked smaller, pitch-soaked lengths of wood around his legs, as high as his knees.

Two priestesses came forward and poured buckets of hot pitch onto the stacked wood. They were careful not to splash too exuberantly. Such a display would never do.

The pitch tasted bitter in the air.

Her Beatitude, the Most Blessed Thora, Mother Metropolitan of the Inland Empire and the Holy Oregon, was resplendent in her robes. She strode forward and stood before the unlit pyre.

It was then that Vlod noticed an Asian moving among the members of Thora's retinue. He was dressed in old hunting clothes, a brown-and-gray wool cloak draped across his shoulders. It, too, looked as though he'd owned it for many, many years. He wore two katana. Both were housed in featureless black scabbards.

No one seemed to take any notice of him, but he appeared to move wherever he wished, unobtrusively shadowing the Mother Metropolitan, but never in such a way that he would draw attention to himself.

It was only because the Asian had moved slightly before the Mother Metropolitan had that he had drawn Vlod's attention.

Thora looked up at Vlod's father. "Do you have anything to say, heretic?" she demanded. She had raised her voice to a near shout, and the strain was too much for her vocal cords. She sounded more like a petulant child than the religious leader of the millions of souls dwelling in the Columbia River basin.

"May I ask a question?" Vlod's father asked. His voice was little better than a croak. Blood drooled from his mouth, and several of his teeth were missing, beaten out. Bruises mottled his face, giving it its only color, apart from the trails of blood. Many of the bruises were dark, but an equal number had begun to yellow.

"By all means, Shivananda," Thora said, making a show of using his name, of showing her magnanimity.

"Thank you, Vladika," Vlod's father said, using one of the quasi-familiar, quasi-formal titles for a mother metropolitan. His use of it conveyed no small amount of contempt, of confrontation, of his refusal, even now, to surrender.

As much as Shivananda could, he lifted his head and squared his shoulders. "Where is it?" he yelled, his voice inexplicably strong. "Where is the ash?"

"Mixed into the ground," Morven said excitedly. He was bouncing on his feet. "The same way we mix in the fireplace ash."

"Quiet," Edmund said.

"But I heard from—"

"Hold your tongue," Edmund said.

"Where's the ash?" Thora shouted, sarcastically. "I'm about to send you looking for it." She smiled, very pleased with herself. "You'll have to send us a report! Write us another one of your learned monographs!"

Laughter rippled through the attending members of her court, her men-at-arms, her priestesses and priests, and the judges of the Holy Tribunal for the Defense and Propagation of the Faith.

The laughter faded.

"That's no answer!" Vlod's father said. "Vladika, you cannot answer because you have never seen it!"

"I most certainly have, heretic. It's everywhere around us." She made an encompassing gesture, her arms spread wide. "Everywhere!"

"You're no shepherd, and you're no protector. You're a charlatan and a fraud! You've never found a grain of it!"

"I've never needed to search for it! Unlike you, my dear Shivananda, I have complete faith in the Goddess' revelations of Herself. I have no desire to tempt Her!"

A round of cheering filled the inner ward.

Peering down over the balustrade, Morven said, "Who's the gook?"

Edmund spun him around. "Never use that word again!" Edmund's voice was low and dangerous. "That man is Japanese. He is Master Yokashima, and he could snap you in half with his little finger."

"Our senseis—"

"Are dilettantes compared to him."

Down in the ward, Vlod's father was saying, "Your evasions, Thora, answer nothing. Where is the ash?"

"Never worry. You'll find it soon enough!"

The laughter of Thora's court rattled along the walls.

She snatched a torch from a waiting hand. The hand belonged to a girl. To Vlod, she looked to be about Morven's age, making her twelve. She was dressed in clothes so fine, the weave so tight, the threads so small, the colors so bright, the stitching so exact, that they marked her out as one of Thora's protégés.

"Thank you, Ulricka," Thora said.

"The honor is mine, Your Beatitude," the girl said, and withdrew. She stood away, not alone, but slightly apart, nestled in her finery, cosseted by a tweed cape patterned in dark green and black. A new expression settled on her face. It was neither smug nor prideful, but one of discovery, one of purpose.

Next to her stood Ameretat, the châtelaine of the Châtellenie of Clatsop and Mayger, the châtellenie that coincided with Clan Iredale's lands. Her labrys hung from her belt, the ornate, highly engraved blades shining. Her crosier was a seemingly simpler affair. From a distance, it looked like an authentic shepherd's staff. It was only nearer to that the gold and silver inlays and the enamel work became evident.

Thora held the torch aloft, waving it as though it were a flag.

Her court gasped in anticipation. The moment had arrived. Righteousness was about to be restored, enforced, and spread abroad by the flames and the smoke and the screams. Clearly, so very clearly, they were obeying the will of the Goddess!

Vlod felt Edmund's hand on his shoulder. "Do not react," Edmund said, his voice pitched for Vlod alone. "You'll shame him if you do."

Vlod nodded his understanding, his remembrance of everything that Edmund and Wolfram had drilled into him the night before.

Thora drew herself up. "Heretic! It's time for you to burn!" she shouted, and threw the first torch.

It landed on the top of the ranks of logs, bounced, and came to rest next to Vlod's father's legs.

The pitch caught, slowly at first because of the cold and the rain, but then the flames sprang to life and the smoke rose up, black and thick.

Vlod's father straightened as though he were backing away from the burgeoning inferno about to engulf him.

More torches followed onto the piled wood.

The fire spread. The wood hissed and popped, and the flames, yellow-orange in the cloud-shrouded light, burst upward.

Vlod's father twisted his face away. Reflexively, he jerked and strained against his chains.

To no avail.

It was the desperate thrashing of a man about to die in unimaginable agony, in a fury of rage and defeat.

Bridging the inner ward, the heat warmed Vlod's face.

His father screamed.

And once started, he did not stop.

As the flames climbed up his body, his screams became high-pitched shrieks.

The shrieks echoed from the walls of the inner ward. They seemed to penetrate into the basalt blocks, fouling them.

Thora and her court smiled. Some cheered. Some laughed. And Morven giggled in delight.

Edmund seized Morven's neck and squeezed, digging the tips of his fingers into the soft, yielding flesh. "I'll not tell you again, boy," Edmund said.

Morven wriggled to break free, clawed at his father's hands, but ceased his repulsive giggling.

The flames reared up, and the smoke lifted toward the sky in black, sinuous billows, like house snakes rising from their holes.

Had his father been wrong to act as he had? Wouldn't it have been better if he had kept his suspicions to himself?

And yet, the ash had to be somewhere, all around them in fact, if Vlod were understanding correctly what his father had told him—all around them and in thick pockets beneath the soil.

Nevertheless, the hard truth was that his father was dying for the sake of a metaphysical hunch, for the sake of his intellectual pride.

Could that be true?

Had Thora been right about him?

Vlod's stomach clenched, but he did not throw up.

He caught the pitch-fired stench of the smoke, and he heard, he forced himself to hear, his father's frantic screams.

They were useless to him, but they were completely satisfying to Thora and her swarm of bootlickers.

The back of Vlod's throat stung. It threatened to close, and his nose felt as though it were on fire. He could barely see.

He refused to give in, to cry, to wail, to provide Thora with the satisfaction of his grief. It was exactly as Edmund had warned him it would be.

"Look at him squirm," Morven said. "He looks like a burning tent caterpillar!"

Vlod shifted his weight, brought his hand in close, and balled it into a fist.

Edmund did two things at once. He gripped Vlod's shoulder, staying his strike, and he backhanded Morven. The blow sent Edmund's son sprawling.

"On your feet," Edmund said, "and keep your mouth shut. Am I understood? You're enough of an embarrassment as it is."

Blood trickled down from the right side of Morven's mouth, which was now quivering.

The smoke now smelled of burning clothes and burning hair.

"Yes, my lord," Morven said, cupping the side of his jaw.

Edmund placed Vlod's hands palms down on the balustrade.

"There's worse to come," he said.

The lentil stones were rough and cold beneath Vlod's fingers. He drew in a type of solidity from them, from the timeless basalt. He pulled it into himself, and he merged himself into the rock, simultaneously anchoring himself to it.

A magus' trick. A warrior's trick.

The stench of burning flesh filled the inner ward.

Thora's smug laughter rode the flames, the smoke, and the screams.

Vlod's father's eyes had grown glassy with terror, and he was whipping his head from side to side, looking for an escape, seeking relief from the mounting agony.

Thicker and hotter now, the flames rose still higher, hissing. The burning wood crackled.

Deep in the core of Vlod's shock another storm of emotion came to life. If he had been a few years older, fourteen or fifteen, say, Edmund and the others would not have been able to keep him on that balcony.

He would have broken ranks with his clan. He would have drawn his knife and attacked his father's murderer. He would have exacted a terrible vengeance on Thora.

He would have taken her head and put it on a spike above the door to his room, and when it had rotted, when it had begun to stink, when it had become a feast for maggots, he would have thrown it to the dogs.

But because he was not older, and because he was not a fiend, and because he was the son of a magus, and because he was an Iredale, he stood where Edmund had told him to stand and he watched. He watched as Edmund had told him to watch, without flinching, without turning away, without wailing and without tears.

Like a blacksmith joining two pieces of metal, Vlod welded the day into his memory.

He would deal with Morven another day.

For now, his portion was to watch and to remember, to watch and shrink away.

Vlod's father shrieked one final time, hopelessly, raggedly, surrendering to the flames, and slumped in his chains. They tore at the charred remains of his clothes, at his blistered flesh, baring it in places to the bone, white and bloody.

"He's gone," Wolfram said, and drew Vlod closer to him. "A finer, braver man never lived."

Vlod wanted to respond, but he couldn't. He promised himself to answer when he could, when his answer would be more than the whimpers of a frightened child, the son of a man executed for heresy.

Two

Because Vlod had listened and watched, because he had not fallen into the trap of his own wretched dismay, he was able to remember the whole of it, from the crunch of the Mother Metropolitan's boots on the paving stones, to the self-righteous expressions on the faces of the members of the Holy Tribunal, to the odor of the ash of his father's execution

It drifted down, and clung to their cloaks. It formed a gray-black paste on their hair. It grimed their hands, and it ran down their faces. It insinuated itself between their tightly closed lips, and it gritted between their teeth, like sand at a picnic on the beach.

Vlod remembered other things, too.

Wolfram's solidity.

Morven's glee.

Thora's smug contempt for Clan Iredale.

Above all, Vlod remembered that Edmund, his father's closest friend, had been powerless to prevent any of it.

The storm revived and drove in from the Pacific Ocean. The squalls and the clouds funneled up the Columbia River valley, and where they couldn't move inland, they piled up against the Coast Range and laid siege to it.

The rain hammered down. The drops, huge and frigid, near to freezing, rattled like thrown gravel where they hit the paving stones. The drops hissed as they struck the flames, sending up tiny puffs of steam.

The blackened corpse fell forward, bending as much as the chains would allow, as though it were acknowledging Thora's victory.

Men-at-arms, Iredales, not the Mother Metropolitan's men, threw bundles of dried branches and further buckets of pitch into the flames.

Execution had become cremation; contempt had become honor.

The change was lost on Thora and her court; otherwise, she would not have allowed it.

The Iredales knew it for what it was.

The flames, ravenous and greedy, howled up. They made a guttural roar. They piled up until they fully encased Vlod's father, until they shielded him from the Holy Tribunal's delight.

The renewed heat bathed Vlod's face, and the stench of the smoke lessened as the fire grew hotter.

As if in answer, the rain fell harder still. It soaked through Vlod's winter cloak and through his tunic, and he shivered.

Edmund touched Vlod's shoulder. It was the slightest of pressures, but it was strong and guiding, not to be ignored. "It's over," the chieftain said. "Come away."

THREE

The wind swept in over the docks. It ruffled the puddles and tugged at Vlod's cape.

Anxious to catch the flood, Thora and her chittering, chattering, perfumed retinue had quit the castle long before the pyre's flames had begun to lower. They had returned aboard their stately galleys, with their bright gilding and their garish paint.

Then, amidst a chorus of bellowed commands, often frantic, the ships had cast off and headed back upriver.

Edmund had gone down to the port to see Thora off. He had taken Vlod with him, but he had left the rest of his family behind, out of view and out of mind.

Standing beside his chieftain, Vlod watched the toylike ships.

They had made a grand sight, out there on the river, a tableau of temporal and religious power, of unrivaled opulence. Their decks bristled with Thora's men-at-arms, with her courtiers, and with her priestesses and priests.

They were happy to be leaving, anxious to be away from the grim coastal weather and from the unschooled, rustic coastal populace. Dour and unwashed. Surly. Did they never bathe? Did they never smile?

The Mother Metropolitan and her court were eager for their next coup, for their next diversion, for their next entertainment.

Their sodden clothes reminded Vlod of a flower garden after a heavy spring rain has beaten down the brightly colored petals.

Where, Vlod wondered, would they all sleep? How would they dry their clothes?

The ships recaptured his attention. The white-painted oar blades, red-tipped, flashed in the meager sunlight.

With the wind strong and fair, the captains set their sails. Normally, these sails were enormous rectangles of brightly striped canvas, but today the captains had reefed them down to thin bands of cloth. They looked like flags, like colorful buntings rather than like sails.

No Iredale captain would have reefed down so far, not on that course, not in that wind, coming as it did from astern. Then again, no Iredale captain would have been caught dead in a ship with such a flimsy rig. Even the clan's fishboats were more heavily built. No, the Mother Metropolitan's vessels were playthings. They were not ships.

Nevertheless, their sails took the strain and drove the matchwood baubles against the river's implacable current, tide or no tide.

The water was brown with silt and littered with pieces of wood, driftwood logs, and, here and there, whole trees, including the roots and branches.

Thora's captains would have their hands full, piloting their ships.

With the wind opposed to the current, a tall, steep chop had built up, a chop decorated with whitecaps. The ships shouldered through it, rising and falling, rolling from side to side. When they came off the tops of the underlying swells, their bows threw aside great spreading wings of foam.

Vlod could sense the rise and fall of the ships as though he were aboard one of them. The movement of the holystoned decks, the way in which each successive wave lifted the ship and then pushed her on, the slight roll to port or to starboard as the swells passed beneath her hull. The motions reached out to him, touched him in a way that nothing else ever would.

But Vlod was not aboard one of those ships, and he had no wish to be. The planks beneath his feet were the planks of the dock on which he stood. There were gaps between the planks, and below them were the massive timbers that gave the dock its shape and strength, its solidity. For the present, it was enough.

Decades of rain and salt had long since scoured away the heady odor of the creosote, but the creosote was still there, ensuring the longevity of the wood.

Nevertheless, sooner or later, the wood would rot out, and when it had, the destroyed pieces would be excised and burned, the ash dumped onto a patch of fill.

Even before the rotten wood had been set alight, the carpenters would have nailed, or screwed, or bolted new planks, new timbers, new wood into the places vacated by the old.

The pilings were another story. The rotten ones would be cut off at low tide, and new ones driven into the river bottom to replace them.

Out on the river, the Mother Metropolitan's ships staggered into their places for the run upstream. They dressed their lines as best they could, on the fly. They had no time to dally over the niceties.

Their timekeepers' drums pulsed over the water.

The drums were made of hide and copper. Each was unique, each sounded a different note, and each was struck in its own manner, but each had the same dual purpose: to set the pace for the rowers and to hold them in time.

The flotilla's sails were drawing, but the rowers would work no less.

Thora's life was one of unrelenting urgency. The sun never paused in his journey across the sky. The moon never rested from her work. The Wheel of the Year never slowed in its turning.

Make haste. Make haste. The day is far spent, the night approaches, and we have far to go. Make haste!

When Edmund had lingered long enough, when he had fulfilled the demands of piety and etiquette, he turned away. His boots grated on the planking.

Vlod walked beside him, back up the hill to the castle.

Vlod's mouth tasted of ash.

Sooner than Thora had expected it would, the salon aboard her galley had grown oppressive.

The afternoon was nearly spent, the tea had gone cold, the food was too sweet and too heavy, and the chatter was like broken glass. The timekeeper's beat boomed through the galley and thudded along the planking, while, not to be outdone, the wind as good as howled in the rigging.

It was, Thora thought, a unique sound: neither a shriek nor a moan and not loud enough to be called a genuine howl. During the stronger gusts, the note climbed up the register. It was as though the ship herself were trying, perhaps, to sing Shivananda's name into the *Dirge*.

Why couldn't he have moved on to another line of research? Why had he insisted on challenging the Great Winter?

The galley's pitch and roll had led to several cases of seasickness, and although many of its pasty-faced victims had made it out on deck to vomit over the side, many had not. Servants had cleaned the salon sole, but the stench lingered, as it always did. Opening the ports offered next to no improvement.

Thanks to the vagaries of the stove and its chimney pipe, the salon was either too hot or too cold. It was always too smoky.

Enough!

Thora decided it was time for her to get out of the whining fug and clear her mind.

She put on a dry cloak and went out on deck.

The sky was low, dense, and gray. The wind, which was coming from astern, was sharp and wet and strong enough to roll over the tops on the wave crests, creating whitecaps. It wasn't outright raining, though, but neither was it dry.

It was, Thora thought, a perfectly miserable afternoon—neither fair nor foul. Foul, truly foul, would have been a distinct improvement.

Up on the poop deck, in addition to the maneuvering watch, she found Master Yokashima, the captain of her personal guard, and the galley's captain. The galley's captain was also serving as the flotillas' commodore. The three of them had their telescopes trained at the nearer shore, the river's southern bank.

Thora joined them.

"What's afoot?" she asked, and held out her hand.

The galley's captain filled it with his telescope. "Riders, ma'am. They've been tracking us."

"Where away?" she asked, and lifted the glass, an excellent specimen, to her eye.

"See that clump of dogwoods? Next to the maples? They're back in there," the galley's captain said. "Three or four of them."

"Five," Yokashima said.

The glass was excellent, the sort reserved for special occasions. The water, the beach, the mud bank, the trees, and the underbrush sprang into sharp clarity.

She tracked the glass back and forth, back and forth, small movements, nothing grand, nothing— And there they were. At long intervals. Far back in the trees.

Three of them.

Four.

And...yes, there was number five. Afoot. Leading his horse. A bow slung across his back.

"A hunting party?" she asked.

"Maybe," the galley's captain said.

"I'd rather we weren't on the menu," the captain of Thora's personal guard said.

Thora returned the captain's glass.

He rescanned the shoreline. "No, they're not hunting. They're out to use us for target practice, more likely."

"They are not hiding," Yokashima said.

"What? Of course they're hiding," the galley's captain said. "They're using the trees for cover."

"Using the available cover and hiding are quite different," Yokashima said. "No, they have chosen not to make an issue of their presence."

"I don't follow," Thora said.

"They want us to know they are there," Yokashima said, "but neither do they wish to make a show of force."

"A show of force?" the guards captain asked, incredulously. "With five?"

"They could have greater strength, farther back in the trees."

Yokashima added, "Five skilled warriors can defeat an army."

"Five?" the ship's captain asked, challenging the assertion.

"I've seen it done," Yokashima said.

Thora didn't doubt his word. She'd heard reports about the man, the sort of reports that left a mark on the memory. They were reports of small determined parties, narrow mountain passes, and great slaughter, tales of meadows carpeted with swords run into the ground and heads driven onto the upright handles.

"Yes, very well," Thora said, "but what are those five up to?"

"Impossible to say," Yokashima said. "The tactic is often used to distract."

"I'm not that easily distracted."

"No, ma'am," Yokashima said, and offered her a respectful nod of his head.

FOUR

As the late afternoon collapsed into dusk, the rain again eased into a drizzle. The remains of the pyre had burned well down, and they were burning lower and lower still. The wind scattered the trails of smoke, and the tiny puffs of steam had gone into hiding. From the edges of the fire, a coarse, black slurry snaked across the paving stones and trickled into the drains.

Shortly before sunset Vlod slipped away and descended into the inner ward. The walls glared down at him, watching, expectant, but otherwise he was alone or nearly so.

The winter cold pierced his cloak, and the drizzle made a half-hearted attempt to soak through his clothing. His boots, however, were wet through, and his feet were numb. The ward smelled of wet basalt and the tar-heavy smoke of the torches. They were being lit now, one by one, to meet the advancing night, to hold the darkness at bay beyond the castle walls.

The air itself, however, smelled clean again.

Vlod stared, dry-eyed, at the place where his father's stake had stood. Scattered in the gray powder were blacker, heavier clumps.

Were those pieces of charred wood, or were they pieces of his father's corpse?

A man-at-arms poked the tip of her spear into one of them. She lifted it and turned it, as though poking at a hearth fire. The clump shattered into falling clusters of red and yellow embers.

Wood, then.

One by one, the embers faded, leaving behind a scattering of charred husks.

Husks.

Not even that much was left of his father.

The Mother Metropolitan's annihilation of him had been complete.

For all time.

For *all* time...

Vlod's resolve collapsed, and he began to cry.

He did not weep or sob or bawl or shriek, but tears welled in his eyes and ran down his face. They stung, hot and freezing at the same time.

Setting aside her spear, the man-at-arms used a long-handled rake to gather a small collection of partially burned pieces of wood. As she made the pile larger, flames appeared. Hesitant at first, they gained strength and danced higher.

Wolfram came and stood next to Vlod, towering above him. The battlemaster put his arm around Vlod's shoulder, further dwarfing and encompassing him.

"Have you come here to feel sorry for yourself, or to mourn your father?" Wolfram asked.

"Was he a heretic?" Vlod asked.

"They burned him for heresy."

"That's not the same thing."

Silence. Then, "Why are you here?"

"Why did they do that to him?" Vlod asked, forcing back his emotions.

"He spoke out of turn."

"How? By asking about the ash?"

"Why are you here?" Wolfram asked again. "To feel sorry for yourself or to mourn your father?"

"To mourn my father."

"Then make it your business to stay alive," Wolfram said.

"What about the ash?"

"Never mind the ash. Stay alive."

"Yes, sir," Vlod said.

He knelt down and filled his pouch with ash.

The light was gone by the time the Mother Metropolitan's ships pulled in close to a sandy beach and anchored. The anchor watches stayed aboard and picket boats were assigned to patrol, but otherwise the crews and the Mother Metropolitan's court went ashore.

The five riders had not been seen since the light had begun to fail. Nevertheless, the ships' crews and Thora's personal guard established an enhanced perimeter. That done, they pitched camp.

The rain had petered out, but the ground was soggy. Complaints and counter-complaints made the rounds.

When wasn't it soggy along the lower stretches of the river?

True, true, but wet or not, bivouacking ashore was better than trying to sleep aboard, cooped up like chickens.

Worse than chickens.

The fires will be especially welcome.

We could use 'em to roast a few chickens, eh?

Bugger the chickens, shipmate. I'm drying my boots.

Miraculously, Thora's people found enough dry and semi-dry wood to build roaring bonfires and enough flat or semi-flat ground to pitch their tents. Two or three of these were elaborate contraptions, but most were low-ceilinged, one-room affairs.

Surprising many, Thora had chosen to stay aboard her galley, but she had sent Aelfled, the aging Crone of the Cathedral, ashore.

The crew had been called upon to help her down into the launch, and even then, she'd nearly fallen. Into the water or into the bottom of the boat, it would hardly have made the slightest difference. At her age, a tumble that most people would laugh off meant broken bones and, quite possibly, a long and miserable death. The other option, falling overboard, could have just as easily meant drowning or death by hypothermia.

Thora didn't like the idea of a new crone, but it was probably time,

time and past, for Aelfled to retire and don the black robes of a cloistered nun.

Perhaps not this year, but no later than next. First, however, a successor would have to be found.

The next Crone of the Cathedral would have to be someone with enough intelligence to advise on matters of policy, enough backbone to stand her ground in an argument, and enough sense of her own calling not to attempt to live through the mothers metropolitan she would serve.

Fortunately, Thora had already identified several possibilities.

She promised herself that when the time came, Aelfled would be accepted in a community as a Rassophore nun, rather than forcing her to begin her monastic life as a novice.

She might find the life of a novice irksome. She was, after all, the Crone of the Cathedral, which was no small thing. She already knew more about theology, spirituality, and liturgics than the rank and file of monastics ever would.

Master Yokashima had asked permission to go ashore.

"Those riders have not left us," he said. "I would like to question them about their intentions."

The thought of Master Yokashima questioning anyone sent a chill slithering down Thora's back.

"I'd rather you stayed aboard," she said. "I've staked myself out like a tethered goat. Let's see who comes calling."

"Very wise," Yokashima said, and left her.

He prowled the ship like a tiger on the hunt, but he made it appear as though he were restlessly wandering from place to place.

Thora had also kept the ship's cook. He was glad to have only a few to cook for, simple fare, too. The last thing he was in the mood for was trying to feed a crowd that was cold, wet, tired, and short-tempered. They ought to have anchored and gone ashore hours earlier, during daylight, but the captains and her high-and-mighty-ness had decided otherwise.

Oh, well. The galley fires were lit and the place was warm. He could cook on an iron stove. Cooking over an open fire befuddled him.

Aboard, too, was the priest Jinhai, also at Thora's request.

Jinhai's formal style was His Honor, the Venerable Jinhai, Archdeacon, Protopriest, and Archthurifer of the Cathedral Henge of Eileen the Immortal. And, just as he was a man of many titles, he was also a man of many talents.

Centuries ago, the Cathedral's archdeacons had been chosen to preside over the civil and criminal trials of provincial clergy. Therefore, the archdeacons were also judges, hence the styles "his honor" and "your honor."

Jinhai despised the honorific and found the work burdensome, but he had made his peace with both. The title, as silly as it was, opened doors, and the work brought him into frequent contact with Thora.

She poured the two of them glasses of Van Horn Butte Reserve, a whisky that was no small refuge when the weather was foul.

They sat at a table in the salon. The space was deserted. The only sound was the tread of the watchstander's boots on the poop deck—side to side and poop-deck rail to taffrail.

"It's too stinking cold in here," Jinhai said.

He built up the fire in the stove, adding the crackle and pop of the burning wood to the muted thud of the pacing on the deck above them.

He sat down and finished his whiskey.

Thora refilled their glasses.

"I envy your skill with a fire," Thora said. "I can barely persuade dry kindling to catch."

"Where I grew up you were either good with a fire or you got beaten until you were." Jinhai sipped his drink. "My grandmother taught me."

Shifting the ground slightly, Thora said, "Thurifers. You're pyromaniacs at heart."

It was an ancient joke, universally declared hoary centuries before the Great Winter. Still, Jinhai smiled at it. "Guilty as charged," he said.

As indeed he was. He'd started out as a boat boy in one of the shrines of a minor clan. He'd applied himself to his duties, kept himself personable and nonthreatening, virtually invisible, and had eventually worked his way up to being a novice thurifer at the Cathedral. Seminary and ordination had followed.

"Aelfled will be retiring soon," Thora said.

"She'll despise monasticism."

"It can't be helped."

"No, it can't," Jinhai said. Nudging the conversation along, he asked, "Who do you have in mind?"

"Either Tatenda or Shabnan would be fine, but I'm leaning toward Glynis."

She sounded fragile, the words rushed, as though she were about to collapse.

Abandoning their conversation, Jinhai said, "You've had a miserable day."

The color drained from Thora's face.

"I'm all right," she said, too defensively.

"No, you're not. You're worse than tired," Jinhai said. It had been cruel to remind her of what had happened at Olney Castle, but Thora couldn't afford to exhaust herself. "You ought to be in bed."

Thora's face hardened. The dam had cracked, but that was the most that it would ever do. It would never break. "I had to burn him," she said, "and I had to pretend to despise him."

"Of course you did. No one questions that. Not even his friends."

"I do," Thora said. "I question it." Her voice was as tight as a drawn hunting bow. "He had the finest intellect I've ever seen."

"Yes."

"I ridiculed him, and I did my best to undercut and humiliate him." Her eyes brimmed over. "Wasn't burning him enough?"

"You had to discredit him. Publicly. He left you no choice."

"No, he didn't," she said, her voice nearly breaking. "Damn him!"

"Personally, I wouldn't go that far, but—"

"Well, I have."

"Yes, you have. You, acting as the Mother Metropolitan, had to."

"Did I? A mind like that? I ought to have found—"

A horn sounded from ashore. It was blaring the wavering, staccato notes of an alarm.

They rushed out on deck and up onto the poop.

A watchstander offered Thora a glass, but she didn't need it to see what was happening. The bonfires and torches provided ample clarity.

About a dozen riders had burst through the perimeter and into the camp. They were hacking down anyone they could reach, anyone who dared oppose them. Several of the riders carried bows, and their arrows buzzed like enraged yellowjackets.

Shouts and screams rose from the camp, rose thicker than the smoke from the bonfires.

The galley's captain came up onto the poop, with Yokashima a half step behind him.

Changing her mind, Thora took the glass.

She had it trained and focused just in time to see one of those streaking arrows bring down the captain of her personal guard.

Among the anchored ships, the pickets drew in closer.

The captain yelled at the watchstanders to watch the deep water. "They'll come out of the black!"

A particularly shrill shriek rose above the tumult ashore.

Then, at the precise moment the attack could have broken the back of the defense, a signal rocket raced aloft, whistling. It burst, sending down a red flash and, less than a second later, a concussive *BANG!*

Instantly, the riders wheeled their mounts away from the encampment and rode downriver, toward Edmund's lands.

———

At dinner that night in Olney castle, the only relief came from the Mother Metropolitan's absence. The food was intentionally plain, but hot, and the meat was fresh, rather than smoked or salted.

The whale-oil lamps gave off their bright, warm light, but the shadows in the corners of the room seemed darker.

The log fire on the grate held the January chill at bay but could not cancel it out.

No one seemed to notice either the lamps or the fire.

Dagna and Brenna chattered, but their piping voices fell off into an uncomprehending silence.

Vlod had changed into dry clothes and boots, but despite them, he was shivering. His teeth weren't chattering, but he felt as though his muscles would never stop trembling. Eating was impossible.

Edmund and Annoria didn't speak beyond the necessities of marshaling four children through a meal, and Wolfram, whose wife had died years ago, said next to nothing, his face set in a resolved stare that spoke volumes.

Morven, Edmund's son and heir, wolfed down his food and, with his father's permission, ran from the table. His boots rapped down the hallway, deeper into the keep.

Brenna and Dagna picked at their food, and when they'd eaten enough for appearances' sake, Annoria excused them.

A moment later, she turned to Vlod. "You may leave if you wish."

"Thank you, ma'am," he said, and went in search of Morven.

———

After trying the stables, the armory, and the kitchen, Vlod caught up to Morven in his room.

It was a comparatively large space, with tapestries hung on the walls and draperies hung over the windows and door. A braided rug covered the floor.

Morven was kneeling on the rug, working on a meter-tall model of a trebuchet. It was meticulous work: cutting, fastening, gluing, ensuring that the reality matched the drawings, that the model would in fact work.

Morven's head snapped up. "What you want, crybaby?"

Without answering, Vlod darted across the room and backhanded Morven across the face. A kick would have been easier and certainly more damaging, but the backhand served far better as the challenge it was meant to be.

Morven gaped, unbelieving, outraged. A blow! His mouth opened and closed like the mouth of a landed carp. His nostrils pumped like gills. His hands, still holding a cross brace and a glue-loaded brush, shook with rage.

"You look just like a burning caterpillar," Vlod said.

"You fucking runt!" Morven snarled, and sprang at Vlod.

Vlod hadn't expected an all-out, direct attack, not immediately, and found himself forced to give ground, to back out through the door, which he had not bothered to close.

The two boys tangled in the draperies, ripping them from the rod.

Morven's much larger size, his sheer weight and greater strength, threatened to overpower Vlod, who stumbled backwards.

He caught his heel on the edge of the carpet runner in the passageway and fell.

The two of them ended up rolling on the floor.

Vlod broke free, and they both scrambled to their feet.

They circled, looking for an opening, for the next line of attack, and then Morven rushed in, throwing a whirlwind of blows.

Morven's fists connected, over and over, despite Vlod's attempts to protect himself, and he was again forced to give ground.

He cursed himself for a fool. He ought to have anticipated Morven's original attack, ought to have sidestepped rather than meeting it head on. Then, in the passageway, Vlod ought to have been the one to attack, ought to have been the one to drive Morven back.

Vlod threw his own punches, but few of them landed squarely and none of them landed with effect.

Vlod's face was beginning to feel like a piece of badly butchered meat, and he could feel the hot, wet stickiness of his blood coursing from a cut on his lower lip and running down his chin. He was shaking now, as though he were suffering from a paroxysm of terror.

He wasn't.

What he was feeling was what he had felt earlier in the day, when the torches had begun to fly: impotent rage.

"Who's the caterpillar now?" Morven bellowed. "Uh? Uh? Weakling! You should have died the day you were born."

Vlod planted his right foot, and using it for leverage, he propelled himself forward.

As he charged, he stooped and lowered his left shoulder.

It was a basic blow, rudimentary, easily deflected, but basic or not, it connected with Morven's solar plexus, that sensitive junction of nerves just below the sternum, and drove into those nerves just as Vlod had hoped it would.

The older boy's mouth opened silently, as wide as though he were about to vomit, and his eyes flashed huge with shock and pain. He gasped like a gutted fish, and then he dropped into a tight ball. He tried to catch his breath, but he couldn't, not yet. It was as though he were learning how to breathe again.

Vlod stood over him.

Morven was rocking back and forth.

"Yes, they exposed me when I was born," Vlod said, "but I survived. Will you, caterpillar? Will you, maggot?"

As savagely as he could, Vlod drove the toe of his boot into Morven's side. The older boy managed to moan, managed to gag, managed to pull himself into a tighter ball.

The blow was a parting gift, a little something for Morven to remember Vlod by.

Vlod turned to leave.

Wolfram stood in the center of the passage, hands on hips, eyes narrowed, face set.

The chieftain's battlemaster arched an eyebrow.

Vlod said, "He insulted my father."

Wolfram nodded. "And *his* father is the one man who stands between you and death."

"I am of the magi," Vlod said.

Wolfram slapped Vlod, hard across the face. It was like being struck with an iron bar. The blow snapped Vlod's head to one side, instantly, remorselessly. Any harder and it would have broken his neck. Any gentler and he would, in time, forget it. His ear rang and his face burned.

"Your father was of the magi," Wolfram said. "You are nothing."

The clan's battlemaster then backhanded Vlod.

Both sides of Vlod's face were burning now, and both of his ears rang like manic alarm bells, shrill and hysterical.

Vlod had never experienced such complete clarity.

Wolfram said, "The kick was unnecessary, and for that you will apologize."

Vlod immediately turned to Morven. "I apologize—"

"Not to him, you arrogant little shit!"

"To whom then?"

"To your way-masters."

FIVE

They took the dead and the wounded aboard Thora's galley. They wrapped the dead in sailcloth and mattress ticking and placed them in an orderly row on the forecastle. They treated the wounded in the salon. A handful of the wounds would prove to be fatal, in a few minutes or in a few days, depending, but the rest amounted to shallow cuts, nasty bruises, a broken arm, and one concussion.

Ulricka, the girl who'd handed Thora the torch earlier in the day, was an in-between case. An arrow had lodge in her right thigh, side to side, with the head protruding.

The attending field medic handed her a glass of the alcoholic tincture of opium. "Drink this," this the medic said.

"What in hell is it?" Ulricka asked.

"Medicine," Thora said.

"For what?"

"It's for me," the medic said. "I don't want to have to listen to you scream."

"I don't scream."

"Lucky us," the medic said. "Bottoms up. I've got seriously wounded people to look after."

"Drink it," Thora said, not sure whether to be proud of the girl or irritated with her. "Now!"

Ulricka drank the opium. Her head went mushy, and they put a leather-padded dowel between her teeth.

"It'll help with the pain," the medic said.

Ulricka tried to speak, tried to tell them to "Go to hell!" but between the opium and her mouthful of leather she couldn't make herself understood.

Thora understood her, though. She tried not to laugh.

"It's better than cracking a tooth," the loblolly said. "You have such pretty teeth. It would be a shame to lose one."

The arrow was removed by parting the shaft between Ulricka's leg and the fletchings, as close to the flesh as possible, and then pulling the remaining part of the shaft, the part with the arrowhead attached, on through.

Good to her word, Ulricka did not scream. Rather, she spit out the leather-padded dowel and let fly a string of curses that would have embarrassed a longshoreman.

The predawn light had spilled across the river, pushing back the night. Revealed was a day of thick clouds, interspersed with swatches of blue. The wind had moderated. Throughout the midday hours there would be next to none at all. It was the sort of day on which the weather might think about raining but on which it seldom delivered any. It was like an alcoholic's promises to reform: lots of talk, but no action.

Up on the poop deck, away from prying eyes and cocked ears, Thora met with the galley's captain, Jinhai, Yokashima, Aelfled, and the acting captain of Thora's personal guard.

Aelfled had been up the whole night, attending to the wounded. She looked both younger than she had in years and, paradoxically, as though she were about to have a stroke and pitch over the nearest rail.

She wasn't alone.

No one aboard had slept, but now that they'd taken the situation in hand, those off watch could at least doze if an opportunity presented itself.

"Why did any of us survive that attack?" Thora asked.

She was met with weary, puzzled looks. The only one who seemed to understand her question was Master Yokashima.

"Because we were not attacked," he said, simply.

"How can you say such a thing?" Aelfled said. "We have dead and wounded!"

"It was a raid, not an attack," Yokashima said. "A force of any appreciable size could have annihilated us. The intent was to harass, not to engage."

"Why?" Thora asked.

"For the shear hell of it," the galley's captain said.

"I tend to agree," Thora said. "Who, then?"

"We took no prisoners, and they left none of their dead or wounded behind," Yokashima said. "We have no way to determine who conducted the raid."

"I should have let you go ashore last evening."

"If you had, you might be among our dead," Jinhai said.

"True," Yokashima said. "They couldn't reach you, so they settled for making trouble."

"Could it have been a Brethren raiding party?" the acting captain of Thora's guard ventured. "Dressed like clansmen?"

Thora shook her head. "Unlikely. They wouldn't have bothered." The Brethren consisted of fallen-away clansmen, the fanatical followers of various snake cults and shamanic traditions, and dozens of seminomadic, largely animist bands. As a body, they were as violent as they were primitive, as vicious as they were disdainful of the Goddess and the God.

"Edmund's people?" Aelfled asked. "He's the sort of illiterate who revels in this sort of stunt!"

"Or someone wanting us to *think* it was Edmund," the galley's captain said, speaking for the first time. "False colors."

"Or true colors trying to look false," the acting captain of Thora's guard said.

They were going in circles, and the Manor Island, Seldon's domain, was hours away. Perhaps Seldon, the chieftain of Clan Sauvie, could provide a few scraps of useful information. If anyone had his ear to the ground, it would be Seldon.

"The unvarnished fact is, we don't know," Thora said, bringing the conversation to a close. "Captain, get us underway as soon as possible."

"Aye, aye, ma'am."

Three days after the Mother Metropolitan's departure, a dispatch rider arrived from Seldon, the chieftain of Clan Sauvie. The rider brought word of a hit-and-run attack on Thora's flotilla. The ships were recouping behind Seldon's walls, but were expected to resume their journey upriver in four or five days. They had wounded who needed attending.

"Their dead will need pickling, too," Wolfram said.

Edmund tossed the dispatch onto his deck. "She'll think we did it," Edmund said. "Did we?"

"No," Wolfram said.

Edmund repeated his question, this time with the sort of emphasis that signaled he would brook no evasion. "Did we?"

"No, we did not."

"Then who did?"

To this, neither of them could formulate an answer.

"I'll ride upriver and take a look at the site of the raid," Wolfram said.

"You won't find anything."

"It'll be worth the effort. If we don't investigate, we'll look guilty," Wolfram said. "We aren't, are we?"

Edmund scoffed at this reversal. "No, we're not, more's the pity."

Vlod had apologized to his way-masters. They had accepted his apology and had introduced him to the horse stance as a means to cultivate endurance and self-control.

Vlod's training proceeded apace, encompassing now the use of the rapier and guarding dagger.

Morven kept his distance. Whether this was out of respect or because he was biding his time, Vlod could not tell. Whatever the case, Morven's was a welcome absence.

Wolfram's trip upriver revealed nothing but disturbed ground and the remnants of dead bonfires and destroyed tents. Thora's people, Wolfram assumed, had collected the spent arrows and discarded weapons, hoping, perhaps, to identify their makers.

For his part, Seldon had little or nothing to add. Thora was wildly popular along the lower river, but, inevitably, pockets of envy and hatred existed.

Xenia, Seldon's sister and the secretly acknowledged brains in the family, commented, "Envy can be very powerful. It's rightly called one of the deadly sins."

It was, Seldon continued, returning to his theme, impossible to enforce the discipline of the faith without kicking up resentment.

"These so-called pockets, how large are they?" Thora asked.

"They're tiny and scattered," Seldon said. He wasn't aware of any group large enough or foolhardy enough to have staged the raid.

"Whoever it was, they may as well have slit their own throats," he said.

"If not, then I'll see to it myself," Thora said.

Xenia smiled appreciatively.

Six

Thora's assassins did not come for Vlod during the first year following his father's execution for heresy.

When it came to the raid on Thora's flotilla, she sent out her own people to investigate, but they came back empty-handed. One of them didn't come back at all, but that was dismissed as one of the hazards of a dangerous trade.

Without evidence, beyond rumor and speculation and one missing agent, the search for the people who'd conducted the raid lost momentum and direction and was eventually abandoned.

Besides, the Cathedral Henge of Eileen the Immortal had other concerns to occupy its attention—the Crone's succession.

Aelfled was retired and packed off to a nunnery, as a Rassophore nun. She'd wanted to retire to a small acreage, to take up farming, gathering, and gardening, but Thora had overridden her.

Aelfled would need people around her, people to watch over her. Retired crones always did. What she would not need was the isolation of a farm. That isolation would leave her unoccupied, apart from the physical work, and unoccupied crones tended to be disruptive. They tended to hold on, and that was invariably dangerous.

With application, Aelfled might well be tonsured into the Little Schema or even, were she to live long enough, into the Great Schema itself.

Thora was no monastic and never would be, but that life had a certain undeniable attraction, and she found herself, in many different and subtle ways, envying the mode of life, the spiritual possibilities, Aelfled had ahead of her.

Contrary to expectation, Shabnan was selected to be the next Crone of the Cathedral Henge. Never one to mince words, Tatenda had created too much turmoil and open hostility. She had the right sort of omnivorous intellect and no end of courage, but she was as abrasive as a fish scaler.

The other alternative, Glynis, had turned the job down flat. She was happy as a châtelaine and her châtellenie was happy with her. Her flock needed a shepherdess and she was eager to oblige. She would help out as much as she possibly could, but she'd do so from within the Sobor.

So, Shabnan it was.

As for Vlod, Thora's assassins didn't come in the second year, nor yet in the third.

As the fourth wore on, it began to appear as though Edmund had misjudged, a rarity.

"They won't come," Annoria said, "not at this late date. He's safe."

"You're wrong," Edmund said. "We've managed to buy him a little time. No more than that."

"She can't possibly believe he's planning to avenge his father."

"Can't she? Come to that, can't he?"

"It would be absurd for her to be afraid of a child."

"She isn't afraid of a child," Edmund said. "She's afraid of the man he'll grow into."

"She isn't a monster."

"Isn't she?"

Edmund redoubled Vlod's training. Weapons. Combat. Pen and

paper. Books. Tactics, strategy, and logistics. Dueling. Healing. Assassination. Stealth.

Spatters of each, but sound. Dueling and stealth took pride of place in the curriculum.

Morven complained about privileges being bestowed on a runt, but Edmund told his son and heir to hold his tongue or face the consequences.

———

August.

The weather was warm and dry for the Pacific coast. Days of blue skies traded places with days of high clouds, which in turn traded places with days of impenetrable, beach-hugging fog.

One day, a blue-skied day came around. The wind was nonexistent, and the river was a flat sheet. The water flowed sluggishly and unhurriedly toward the bar, freshwater mixing into salt, shoal water merging into deep.

The sun was high, but the air, having come in off the Pacific Ocean, had an underlying chill to it.

Ships and barges from upriver and oceangoing merchantmen filled the docks, while out on the river a half dozen ships from upriver rode at anchor.

They were waiting their turns to discharge their outward-bound cargoes: wheat, lumber, wool, salted meat, hides, salted fish, silk from the Manor Island, cheese, and mushrooms. Or they were waiting to pick up their upriver-bound loads: salt, Asian silk, coal, cotton, iron, steel, glass, coffee, tea, spices, slaves, tobacco, cane sugar, and religious pilgrims.

Vlod swung around the rowboat he was sharing with Brenna so she could better see the three-masted river galley he'd pointed out to her.

"See her now?" Vlod asked. "She's the *Maid of Pasco*. She's one of the Pasco-Burbank ships."

"How do you know?" Brenna asked.

Vlod swung the boat again, putting the ship off the rowboat's beam. "Only ship she can be," he said.

"We're too far away to read her name."

"Don't need to. See the way her stern swoops up?"

"Lots of ships have swoopy sterns."

"Not like that one." Nor did lots of ships have papyrus and lotus decorations painted along their gunwales.

He rowed toward the ship until her name became legible: *Maid of Pasco.*

"You win," Brenna said.

A launch detached from *Maid* and headed for the port.

When it came to rowing dry, the launch's crew had yet to acquire the knack. The coxswain bellowed curses, threats, and entreaties, but the rowing didn't improve. If anything, it grew worse, stroke by stroke, boat length by boat length.

The launch went by without hailing.

Vlod rowed around *Maid*'s stern.

A kid sat there, peeling carrots. His feet dangled over the water.

"Where're you headed?" Vlod asked.

"I'm not supposed to say," the kid said.

"Ah," Vlod said.

"I bet you don't know," Brenna said.

"I do so."

"Then tell us."

"Can't."

"Who says."

"I do," a man's voice said. It came from an open stern window. "I'm the captain."

"So, Captain, where're you headed?" Vlod asked.

"Shove off, kid," he said, and pointedly closed the window.

When Vlod had rowed them a ways off, Brenna said, "They're gonna try to run the bar."

An image of the murderous swells that often built up in the zone where the outflow from the Columbia River met the Pacific Ocean flashed through Vlod's mind. Those swells, steep and high, combined with the river's shifting channels and the vagaries of wind and weather made the Columbia River bar a dangerous place, even for seasoned hands. For the likes of the captain of *Maid of Pasco*, sound-enough river men, it was the next best thing to a meat grinder.

It was no wonder that Edmund forced outbound ships to have bar pilots, but given the fees those pilots charged, it was also no wonder that no few river captains, off on their first deep-water adventure, often with their egos on their sleeves, tried to head out on their own.

"Yeah, he looks like a bar runner," Vlod said.

"We ought to tell Wolfram."

"We will."

And try *Maid of Pasco* did, that very night.

She didn't make it very far.

The moment she began to shorten her cable, the Iredale river patrol swooped in and demanded an explanation.

Maid's captain was outraged. Explanation? Since when did *Maid* need permission to conduct a perfectly routine maneuver?

The officer in charge of the patrol boat shot back, "What maneuver would that be? The wharfingers haven't assigned you to a berth yet, have they?"

"Well, no. Not as such," *Maid*'s captain said.

Vlod and Brenna, hidden in the patrol boat's bow, tried not to giggle.

"Then where are you headed?"

"We aren't headed anywhere." The captain's tone had slipped from outraged to surly.

"Then why are you hauling up your anchor?"

"I'm not. When we first anchored, we accidently let out too much cable, and now she's swinging uncomfortably. I'm bringing in a few fathoms in the hopes that she'll settle down."

More suppressed giggles.

The officer said, "You know, Captain, I'd hate to think you were trying to run the bar. Do you have any idea how dangerous the bar could be?"

"You don't have any right—"

"I have every right," the officer said, "and the power, too."

"Now you listen to me, punk! I have a right to—"

"Have you ever seen someone who's drowned on our bar?"

"No."

"Well I have. Lots of times. It isn't pretty. For one thing there isn't much left by the time the bodies finally wash up...if they wash up."

"Oh."

"Yes, oh," the officer said. "Now either wait your turn or go back upriver to your sandbars and your mudflats."

"We'll wait," the captain of *Maid of Pasco* promised.

Vlod's martial-arts training did not go to waste.

Between his ninth and eleventh year, the Mother Metropolitan had given every sign that she had lost interest. However, during the year Vlod turned twelve, the attempts on his life began. Either the army or the household guard intercepted and thwarted them, but Edmund and Wolfram saw to it that Vlod was stepped through each of the attempts, was present for the interrogations of the surviving would-be assassins, and was among the witnesses at their executions.

In the late fall of the year Vlod turned fourteen, one of the Mother Metropolitan's assassins evaded the patrols, slipped by the guards, and entered Olney Castle.

Vlod and Brenna, who was now twelve, were playing Hounds and Jackals in the family's sitting room. They were seated at a small table, on camp stools. A couple of meters away, a low fire burned on the hearth. Its light flickered on the tapestried walls and on up onto the floor joists and planking of the chamber above. Tallow dips illuminated the game board, the dice, the hounds and the jackals.

Despite the tea he was drinking, Vlod had to make an effort to concentrate, to keep from dozing. He felt snug and secure, happy to be with Brenna, happy to indulge her passion for the game.

Morven considered it beneath him, let alone spending time with either of his sisters, and Dagna despised the game. To her, it was pointless.

Dagna had yet to figure out that the pointlessness of a game, in and of itself, was what made a game a game, and, therefore, paradoxically, worth playing. In a sense, games were like reality, but without the iron consequences.

Brenna advanced one of her hounds. It was a solid move, not good, not bad. The dice had been kind to her.

"Let's see if you can do any better," she said, and passed the dice to Vlod.

"You can't intimidate the dice," Vlod said. "They have minds of their own."

The faintest of metallic scrapes sounded from behind draperies hanging over the room's main windows. A slight draft followed. It barely disturbed the candle flames. The draft brought with it a hint of night air, heavy with the aroma of fir trees.

Another one of Thora's...enthusiasts. Still, to have made it as far as the window, he was better than most.

Vlod was sitting facing those same draperies. He had the fire to his left. Brenna had her back to the draperies, the fire to her right. The firelight gilded her raven-black hair and picked out the weave of her tunic. It was an old garment, one that Vlod had outgrown.

She grinned at him. "Make it good," she said.

Vlod shook the dice and threw them. He commented on the paucity of the result and moved one of his jackals.

He kept his hands in view. It was a gamble, an invitation, but to have done otherwise would have sent a warning, would have surrendered control of the situation to the assassin lurking on the sill of the now-unlatched window.

An assassin, surely, but not skilled, a beginner.

He was taking far too long. He should have been through the window and had their throats slit by this time. Was he an amateur or a perfectionist?

Why did Thora send them?

Was there a dynamic within her court that forced her to keep them in play?

And speaking of plays, why hadn't he made his?

Perhaps a spur was in order.

"The fire's gone down," Vlod said, glancing toward the yellow-orange flames. "How about another piece of wood?"

Brenna cocked an amused eyebrow. "Fine by me," she said. "Shall I?"

"I promise not to cheat."

"Oh, damn. Where's the fun if you don't cheat?"

She pushed her chair back, causing it to scrape on the floor. She crossed the short distance to the stack of firewood next to the hearth. The firelight glinted on the black leather scabbard of her chamber dagger.

She rummaged among the pieces, a mixture of knotted oak and fir. At length, she selected one.

The only question now was whether she'd throw it at the draperies or add it to the fire.

As though she'd read Vlod's mind, she frowned slightly, frowned without changing her expression, without altering the rhythm of her movement. In the end, she tossed the wood into the flames.

It was better to maintain the pretense than to risk giving their unwelcome visitor an opening. Wolfram would have been proud of her choice.

A welter of sparks flew. Caught in the chimney's draft, they disappeared upward in a sparkling, yellow swirl, comforting and beguiling.

At just that moment, the assassin threw the window wide open, propelling it aside with such force that the glass shattered. In almost the same instant, the man, who was dressed in black from head to foot—aren't they always?—somersaulted into the room. He was a blur amidst the pieces of the shattered window and the folds of the draperies.

It was nicely done, no hint of his having become tangled in the heavy fabric, of being distracted by the broken glass. Vlod had to give the man full marks for his physical skill.

Before the first shards of glass had hit the floor, Brenna had turned into the attack.

Vlod rolled to his right, out of his chair, away from Brenna, and out into the center of the room. At one and the same time, he kicked the table, flipping it over, spilling the game pieces across the floor in a clattering spray of game board, hounds, jackals, dice, and candle stand.

The rug cushioned Vlod's impact, but despite the rug and despite Vlod's tunic, the floorboards gouged into his shoulder. A bolt of pain stabbed down his arm.

His arm?

What had he hit?

No matter.

The assassin came out of his somersault holding a small over-and-under crossbow. The weapon had short steel bows, one on top of the other, both compound-rigged. His right hand was on the rear handle, and his left was on the forward grip, which projected to the side between the bows, like the handle of a reaper's scythe. It was an awkward weapon, but it was no less deadly for its lack of grace. The firelight shone, rather prettily, on the shining, triple-bladed bolt heads.

The assassin sidestepped around the overturned table, looking for an open shot.

Vlod rolled, nothing fancy, a plain battlefield move, farther out into the room, drawing the man farther away from Brenna, distracting him, giving him two widely separated targets, rather than an easy group.

Vlod curled into a ball, not unlike the assassin's somersault, but there the similarity ended. Rather than flipping in the air, Vlod used the move to position himself in a low crouch. He drew his battle knife with his right hand and cocked the weapon over his left shoulder, readying it for a cross throw.

But then the assassin's index finger tightened on the weapon's trigger and his hand flexed on the forward grip.

Vlod dodged away, hoping he wasn't overplaying the move, reacting too quickly.

The slip and twang of the crossbow was instantly followed by the whine of the first bolt. It passed through the space where, a split second before, Vlod's chest had been.

Vlod threw his knife.

It spun in the air and buried in the center of the man's chest.

Less than an eye-blink later, Brenna's chamber dagger sprouted next to Vlod's battle knife. Truly, she was Wolfram's niece as much as she was Edmund's daughter.

The second bolt flew and lodged with a dull report in the floor next to Vlod's knee.

The assassin's body arched and twisted, his eyes gaping as he dropped to the floor.

The man's expression reminded Vlod of the expression on Morven's face, all those years ago, when Vlod had shouldered him in the solar plexus.

Blood flowed across the assassin's chest, and it ran from his mouth. He twitched, thrashed, and went limp. His eyes lost all expression.

Vlod and Brenna stared down at the corpse.

Vlod's stomach contracted violently. "Shit," he said, doubling over and heading for the door. He did his best not to vomit on the carpet, but he failed miserably.

Brenna's stomach, however, was made of sterner stuff.

"Some warrior you are," she commented dryly.

"Your knife was late," he said, more or less gasping out the words.

"I didn't want to unman you."

A second spasm contracted Vlod's stomach. "How sporting of you," he said, and doubled over again.

Was she a cradle warrior?

When Vlod's retching was over, finally, mercifully over, Brenna handed him a cup of water.

He nodded his thanks and sipped it.

"What's wrong?" she asked, not unkindly. "You've seen dead people before."

"This time it was different," Vlod said. "This time the bastard was after me. Personally."

"Eyewash. They've been after you for years. Personally." She cocked her head to one side. "This was the first time you've ever had to deal with one of them yourself. Personally."

"You put a knife in his chest, too."

"Good thing, too."

"Yeah. Good thing."

It was only then that he noticed that his shoulder was bleeding. A glance at the floor where he'd landed revealed a protruding nailhead. It must have been what had ripped into him.

Brenna inspected the wound. "Make it bleed," she said.

"It's a tear, not a puncture."

"Humor me," she said.

"It's already bled a lot."

"Not nearly enough."

"Says you."

"Call me a sadist, but I don't want your arm to rot."

Vlod squeezed around the gash, increasing the trickle of blood. It dribbled down his arm.

Brenna handed him a cloth napkin from the sideboard. "That ought to be enough. Besides, you're making a mess."

Using the napkin, Vlod stopped the flow of blood. The pressure hurt almost as much as the nailhead had.

Brenna pulled their knives from the body, cleaned them on the assassin's clothing. Handing over Vlod's knife, she said, "Maybe now Uncle Wolfie will take me with him into the field."

———

Brenna's formal military training began the next day.

To mark the occasion, Edmund presented her with an heirloom battle knife. It had a steel blade, a silver pommel in the shape of a skull, and elk-horn grip panels.

"It's been in the family for generations," Edmund said. "The last person to carry it in battle was my maternal grandmother."

Brenna held the weapon as though it were a religious relic.

"I remember the stories," she said.

"There're others you haven't heard," Edmund said. Changing tone, he asked, "What about the knife? Do you like it? Does it suit you?"

Brenna carefully drew the weapon from its sheath. She hefted the blade, testing its balance. It was huge in her hand.

"It's beautifully wrought," she said, "and perfectly balanced." She turned the knife one way and then the other, cutting the air.

Vlod fancied he could hear the blade's edge sundering the dust motes.

Then, in one sudden move, she threw the knife, as hard as it made any sense to throw it, at the nearest tree, a thick-trunked cedar. The knife sank deep, as its long-ago armorer had intended it to do.

"It likes you," Edmund said.

Brenna smiled. It was the smile of someone who's found her true calling. "The feeling's mutual."

"Heaven help the enemy," Wolfram commented.

SEVEN

Year by year, Edmund, Wolfram, the clan's magi, and the clan's way-masters instilled in Vlod the powers of life and death, an understanding of medicine and mysticism. They brought him up to be a warrior of Clan Iredale, a warrior and more than a warrior.

It was the safest way.

It was the only way.

Thora never truly gave up. Her outright assaults thinned, but it was a dull year that didn't reveal one or another of her attempts to shadow Vlod's movements, his training as a warrior, his steadily growing range of skills.

And, too, although the attempts on his life thinned, they did not melt away to nothing.

It was as if the spies were meant to distract them from the would-be assassins.

By the time Vlod turned eighteen, by the time decisions had to be made, Edmund had reluctantly concluded that they had not done enough, that their efforts had been largely misdirected, not thrown away, but inadequately focused. Vlod was like a wagon with three wheels, like a ship without a chart.

Brenna was a born warrior, a warrior in ways that Vlod would never be.

Where he was brooding, quiet fog and sudden lightning, she was sunny days and jolly thunderstorms.

Dagna, Brenna's younger sister, was a fair duelist, to the extent that she gave a damn about such things, but she despised the military and had next to no patience with court protocol. She was happiest out hunting or immersed in the rituals of the Iredale's manor henge, Manor Henge of Desdemona the Shipbreaker.

Was it piety or religiosity? A quest for the eternal?

Hardly. For her, it was a matter of esthetics. The rites were nearer to choreographed reenactments of legend than they were to sacramental observances, the sacred writings and theology more akin to sagas and speculation than to expressions of absolute belief. They were uplifting palliatives rather than directives.

Morven, Edmund's son and heir, was another paradox. He loved the army, and he loved skirmishes. He delighted in cattle-raiding. At heart he was a brawler. To him, a battle reduced to a series of one-on-one fights, challenges given and answered. He struggled with tactics, with the movement and engagement of units.

The enemy is right over there. What are we waiting for?

To him, strategy was, as yet, a vague concept.

Why don't we just go out and find the bastards and have done with it? Why build fortifications?

The notion of logistics never entered his head.

Everybody got a sword and a shield? Plenty of spears? Good. Then let's be off. Why bother with supply wagons and pack animals? They'll only slow us down. We can carry whatever we need in our saddlebags, can't we? Food and fodder? Who needs 'em? We can forage on the way.

When it came to Vlod, well, he was a thoroughgoing riddle. Edmund's analogies about wagons and ships helped, but they gave rise to at least as much confusion as insight, and at the end of the day, neither was of much help.

Come to that, did Vlod understand himself, his own motivations?

Edmund doubted it.

Edmund's one certainty was that forcing Vlod to attend his father's execution had been the correct choice. It had lent him iron and the kernel of what might one day grow into wisdom.

As his father had been, Vlod was small in stature, a half a head shorter than Edmund, who was himself shorter than Wolfram.

As Vlod's father had been, Vlod was small-boned, wiry rather than brawny, quick rather than strong, a raider rather than a campaigner.

Vlod had the questing, restless intellect of a true magus, his father's intellect, powerful and honed to a cutting edge, rather than a warrior's straightforward cunning.

On campaign Vlod was unaccountably—some said unsettlingly—deadly, especially when pouncing on an enemy patrol.

Deadly or not, however, a career in the clan's military would not do. Vlod was, or could become, a sharper, subtler instrument.

That cutting edge of his needed honing, and it needed the sort of discipline that life in the clan could not give it.

That said, once that edge had been sharpened by a master...

No wonder the Mother Metropolitan wanted Vlod dead.

Edmund did not. Edmund wanted him very much alive. And yet, Clan Iredale could not protect him indefinitely. In the long run, he would have to protect himself.

Nor could the clan hire a master of the sort required. Vlod would have to go to the master. That *going* would be no small part of the training.

There was, therefore, only one thing for it.

Edmund weighed his options, considered the possible outcomes.

It was, likely, an impossible task, and the training might prove inadequate, and yet, it was the only option available to them.

Nothing else made any sense.

Edmund called Vlod into his study.

The early summer weather was warm and the grate was without a fire.

"Yes, my lord?" Vlod asked.

Edmund decided to make his announcement from behind his desk, which at the moment was littered with papers, including the sketches for the current set of repairs to *Koan*, the chieftain's galley. "I'm sending you to the Academy of Archmagus Basil the Anchorite and Wonder-worker," Edmund said. "You'll freeze your ass off, but it'll make a magus of you."

"A magus?" Vlod had blurted, unable to hide his consternation.

"Yes, a magus. You once famously said, and I quote, 'I am of the magi.' Here's your chance to make good on your boast."

"I was nine years old."

"And now you're eighteen. A decision about your future needs to be made, and I'm making it." Edmund smiled. The expression on Vlod's face was the warp and woof of legends. "Augury, spirit journeys, medicine, mysticism, philosophy, astrology. You'll be enchanted." He laughed at his own pun. "You like books, don't you?"

"They murdered my father," Vlod said.

"Thora murdered your father," Edmund said, his voice cold.

"The magi, too."

"They were complicit, as was I."

"You had no choice. They did."

"I'm giving them a chance to make it good."

"Don't I have any say in the matter?" Vlod asked.

"No."

Edmund was shading the truth. No one could force another to become a magus.

He continued, "We could both pretend that you do, but you don't."

Which, as far as Edmund was concerned, settled the matter.

He added, "Yes, my lad, it's the Academy for you."

"They'll never take me."

Notoriously, the Academy lived by its own rules, made its own decisions. Even the Mother Metropolitan treaded lightly on that ground.

None of which meant that Edmund was without leverage.

He indulged himself in another smile. "They will when they've heard what I have to say to them."

Vlod shrugged. "What am I supposed to do as a magus?"

"For one thing, you might possibly stay alive. For another, if you do, you'll bind up people's wounds, tell fortunes, give sage advice, learn obscure bits of lore, gather herbs and plants by the light of a full moon —the usual mumbo-jumbo."

"Oh."

Vlod didn't sound any too happy at the prospect. No surprise there, but needs must.

"I'd rather serve in the army," Vlod said. "Or I could become a bar pilot. Maybe a shipwright."

Rolling right on by those suggestions, Edmund said, "You'll have to learn how to mutter. In case you haven't noticed it, magi do a lot of muttering."

"Whose fortunes? Whose magus will I be?"

"*Mine.*"

"The Academy would never allow it. Graduates are never sent back to their home clans."

"They'll assign you wherever I tell them to."

Edmund wasn't sure whether he believed that one or not. The words had come out of his mouth, the promise was as good as made, but could he deliver on it?

EIGHT

Three months later, close to sunset on a warm August day, an admissions committee from the Academy arrived in Fort George by packet.

Three men made up the committee. Two of them were magi, but the third, an Asian, was decidedly not. The magi wore rapiers, the signature weapon of the magi, while the Asian contented himself with a katana, which he kept sheathed in a black-lacquered scabbard without ornamentation. The lacquer was faded, due for renewal.

Vlod had seen the Asian, a Japanese, once before, nine years previously. He had been wearing two katana then, rather than one, but apart from a handful of deepened lines, his face was unchanged—the same brown-black eyes, the same neutral expression, the same flowing movements.

For the first time in his life, Vlod was certain that he was about to die.

He had, he told himself, no authentic reason to feel that way, but he did. Try as he might, he could not dismiss the apprehension.

The committee had two servants with them. The first was an old man with grizzled hair. He was of medium height, thin, and had fingers that looked as though they'd been stretched. Apart from a boot knife, he carried no weapon. The other had little to mark him out: medium height, medium build, and hair that he wore gathered into a queue, which he had bound along its length with crisscrossed leather straps.

Eighteen hours later, the three of them were seated behind a trestle table in a tower sitting room. It was an open space with an iron stove, suitable for both heating and cooking. The room also featured braided canvas rugs made from worn-out sails, pale-brown window draperies, and a brightly colored tapestry of hounds bringing down a stag. The draperies had been pulled aside to admit the afternoon light.

Vlod stood before the three, a respectful distance off. He was wearing his battle knife, openly on his hip, and two boot knives. They were not fashion pieces. He had also secreted three other throwing knives within the sleeves and folds of his clothing.

The image of the hounds bringing down a stag did nothing for his sense of self-assurance. Indeed, it convinced him that he should have donned a lightweight mail shirt under his tunic and added a fourth throwing knife.

The two magi were dressed in their academic robes. These were floor-length, black silk garments with bands of color on the sleeves to indicate rank and specialty—blue for augurs, red for medicine, brown for natural history, yellow-orange for astrology, and so on.

Hudson, the magus who chaired the committee, made the formal introductions. The smiles and nods exchanged down on the docks were all to the good—where would they be without them?—but for the business at hand, the traditional proprieties, the strict procedures, had to be followed.

Hudson had four white bands on his sleeves. He taught necromancy and reincarnation and was the dean of the College of Spiritual Arts.

To Hudson's right was Newell, the other magus. He had three green bands on his sleeves. Newell's face reddened as though he were embarrassed at being introduced. He taught mythology, history, and archaeology.

As though restless or merely bored, as though he couldn't bear to sit still another moment longer, the Japanese stood up, nodded casually to Vlod, and went to a window.

The move was too relaxed.

Vlod's mouth was already dry, but it went drier still.

Hudson introduced the Japanese as Master Yokashima, the Academy's master of the martial arts.

Vlod remembered the name, remembered the man, but pretended that he had never seen him before the moment he had landed the previous day.

It was a convenient lie, of course, and Yokashima gave every indication that he didn't believe a word of it. On the other hand, it would do no conceivable good to put it into the open that Yokashima had attended the execution of Vlod's father and that Vlod remembered that Yokashima had.

Yokashima was dressed in the same clothes he had come ashore in. Much as they had been nine years ago, they were working clothes, hunting clothes: trousers, lightweight boots, tunic, and a long jerkin. They were in browns, tans, and grays. Their cloth was coarsely woven, and the leather was old. One of the buttons on his cape was broken.

Apart from size and color, Yokashima's clothes were indistinguishable from the clothes of the old man, their servant.

Yokashima stared out the window.

His posture provided Vlod a view of the man's profile.

He was short, shorter than Vlod, and excessively thin, but not emaciated. His hair was black, but it was also steaked with gray. His skin was tight but deeply lined around the eyes and mouth. No matter the man's chronological age, he had an ancient face.

Taken as a whole, he reminded Vlod of a drawn war bow.

Newell cleared his throat.

With a start, Vlod returned his attention to the two magi.

Managing a tight smile, Newell said, "I had the pleasure of teaching your father. Shivananda was a brilliant student. You have every right to be proud of him."

"Thank you," Vlod said.

Yokashima turned his back to the room, turned his back squarely toward Vlod.

It was an odd thing for the man to have done, to divide himself off so completely from the two magi.

Gesturing politely toward Yokashima, Hudson said, "Master Yokashima, do you have any questions for this candidate?"

Vlod nodded toward the man's back.

Vlod had to concentrate on his breathing to keep it from going ragged and shallow. As it was, the muscles across his chest had tightened to the point of physical pain.

Surely an attack was coming. Would the man never make his move?

Yokashima's cloak was of lightweight gray wool. A three-corner tear marred the fabric halfway down on its right side, and a brownish stain snaked across the hem on the left.

The stain was blood, but was it animal blood or human blood? Was its presence deliberate, an act of braggadocio, or was it an ignored accident of a life lived in the open? Or was it there as an eloquent warning to those who had presence of mind enough to read it?

It was hard to say.

Blood is difficult to remove, and the cloak had the look of an old and favored garment.

Suddenly, Master Yokashima spun back toward the center of the room. As he did so, he hurled a small throwing knife at Vlod's chest.

Using his left arm, Vlod sent the knife flying off to the side. In a compound movement, he drew his battle knife and threw it at Yokashima.

The blade leapt like a dancer across the distance, tumbling, flashing, a living thing. The aroma of the blade's steel and the note of fresh oil played through Vlod's awareness.

Yokashima stood as though he had an unlimited amount of time in which to respond. Indeed, he was reacting, or *not* reacting, as though the passage of time did not apply to him: his body relaxed, his face calm, a faint smile shaping his mouth. He looked as though he were meditating, as though he were a Zen master.

His eyes were black and shining, seeing nothing while seeing everything.

Those eyes—so amused and eager, so entertained—could shatter an opponent.

Then, moving with a timeless grace, Yokashima plucked Vlod's battle knife from the air, as casually as though he had plucked an apple from a low branch.

An instant later, the knife was dancing back across the room.

It appeared that two could play the game.

When the knife had danced close enough, Vlod snatched it from the air and sent it into the floor at Yokashima's feet.

It made a sharp, quavering note and lodged tight.

Yokashima's smile remained as before, giving nothing away.

The game was not over yet.

The old man, the servant, rushed forward and sprang into a flying kick, one leg tucked up beneath him, the other extended.

How was it possible for such an ancient to jump that high?

Simultaneously, the younger servant seemed to fade into the background, to merge into the semi-shadows next to one of the windows.

Vlod parried with his right arm, pivoted, and shoved the man on by with his left. The man landed, rolled like an acrobat, and renewed his attack.

For the next four seconds, an eternity for such a contest, the old man punched and kicked, leapt and dove, swept with his arms and legs. He spun like a racing waterwheel. His hands blurred.

In the end, he and Vlod stood very close, facing each other, their hands raised as though they were short swords, the backs of their right hands nearly touching.

It was the stance normal to the opening of a duel, not its conclusion.

The old man stood as though he were made of stone, unmoving and unmovable.

Vlod matched him.

This was no duel, no routine test. But was it life or death?

Were these two another team of Thora's assassins?

Should Vlod have killed Yokashima when he'd had the chance?

It was a good question, one that led to another. Would it have been physically possible for Vlod to have sent his knife into Yokashima's chest, into his heart?

That question had only one answer: No!

The old man was breathing as though he were sitting in a comfortable chair, but Vlod could feel the heat radiating from the man's body and smell the faint tang of the sweat that had formed beneath his clothes. His face had set into no discernable expression.

"How say you, Sensei?" the old man asked.

"The matter is settled," Yokashima said. "The boy lives."

The old man edged away and slowly lowered his hands.

What had Yokashima meant by "the boy lives"? Was he an assassin who'd unaccountably changed his mind? Was this contest a prelude to a deeper test?

What had Edmund arranged with this master of the martial arts?

No matter the answers, the situation possessed its own dynamic, its own inner rules. The outside world be damned.

Vlod mirrored the old man's move.

The old man inclined his head, more than a nod, less than a bow. "I shall make tea."

"Thank you," Vlod said.

"Not tea," Yokashima said, his voice transparently quarrelous. "I despise tea. Make coffee instead."

"As you wish, Sensei," the old man said, and went to the hearth.

Vlod returned his attention to Master Yokashima.

Both the master's face and his posture were impossible to read. Not so the expressions of the two magi.

Clearly, an issue had been decided.

With an emotion akin to a mixture of regret and pride, Vlod realized that they had decided to admit him to the Academy on the strength of Yokashima's say-so.

But that threw the Academy's hierarchy into disarray. The choice had to be theirs, but unquestionably, they had left it up to Master Yokashima.

Vlod bowed to the two magi. It was a court bow, the gesture of a child of the Iredales to two respected officials.

Then Vlod bowed to Master Yokashima. It was the correct bow, right fist in left hand, one warrior to another. "Master," Vlod said, deliberately using that term as opposed to *sensei*.

Returning the bow and the salute, Yokashima said, "You decline admission?"

"My place is here," Vlod said. At the edge of his field of vision he saw the old man moving toward the sideboard, while the younger servant was moving toward the area of the stove.

"Your chieftain says otherwise," Yokashima said.

"I obey Edmund in all things, but this is my decision to make."

"Then, despite your words, you do not obey him in all things," Yokashima said. "Edmund's permissiveness surprises me, as does your willingness to dishonor him."

"He knows I mean no disrespect," Vlod said.

The younger servant bent over the wood box by the stove, as though preparing to build up the fire to brew the coffee.

"Alas, others will not see this as he does."

The younger servant twisted his right arm, as though reaching for a piece of wood. In and of itself, the move was innocent enough, but then he shrugged his right shoulder, there was a muted click, and a shuriken appeared in his right hand.

Vlod saw the weapon only because he caught the twinkle of light on one of its points.

What happened next took less than a second and a half.

It ended with the younger servant dead, lying on his back, his lifeless eyes staring in frozen terror at the ceiling. Blood trailed from his mouth and chest. It soaked into the rug. He had three knives in the center of his chest. One belonged to Vlod, but the others had come from Yokashima and the old man.

The two magi stared at the tableau, not daring to speak. Their faces were pale and their hands were trembling.

Vlod focused his attention on Yokashima.

The would-be assassin had failed, but the rest of the situation was largely an enigma. Had Thora sent the man, as she had sent so many others, or had another of Edmund's enemies seized an opportunity? How had the man attached himself to the admissions committee? What part had Yokashima played? Who else had been involved? What about the old man?

The questions multiplied. They branched and divided like water courses in a broad delta.

There was nothing of importance that Vlod could ask and nothing of importance that Master Yokashima could answer in front of the two magi.

The entrance to a labyrinth had opened. Within it lay the answers to his father's murder. A simple charge of heresy had not been, could not have been, the whole of it.

In that labyrinth, too, lay the reason behind the repeated attempts on Vlod's life. Thora's possible fear of revenge was not, could not be, the whole of it.

Vlod also had Edmund and Clan Iredale to consider. How many of them would die, how many of them would endure unspeakable dangers to keep Vlod alive?

And more...

Indeed, where was the ash?

Edmund had the truth of Vlod's predicament, and it was pointless at this juncture to deny it. Vlod could not remain as he was. He could not further endanger the clan, nor, now that it had been presented, could he throw away a chance to move forward.

Repeating his bow and the hand-in-fist salute, Vlod said, "Sensei!"

To which Yokashima replied, "Deshi. Welcome to my dojo."

NINE

As Master Yokashima had requested upon his arrival in Fort George, his and his servant's rooms were on the uppermost floor of the residence block above the stables. The building also served as a ready-use storehouse. It shared a common wall with the keep and backed onto the inner curtain wall.

The sitting room was sparsely furnished with the keep's faded discards, including a rug made out of discarded rope. Vlod remembered it as having once been in Wolfram's study. The odors of fodder and horses lent a subtle undercurrent to the aromas of recently brewed coffee and the embers smoldering on the grate. Because of those embers, the room was comfortably warm.

Vlod sat where Yokashima indicated he was to sit, in a straight-backed chair with scarred paint and a wobbly left arm.

The servant served mugs of coffee. The mugs were of the no-nonsense variety, heavy ceramic and without handles. Like the furniture, they were scarred veterans of the keep.

After Yokashima had tasted the coffee and nodded his approval, Vlod sipped appreciatively.

He barely tasted the coffee. Despite his outer calm, his stomach felt knotted and his heart was racing. He could feel the blood pounding in his face and the sweat forming on his hands.

Why had Yokashima invited him? Another test? Was another assassin waiting, out of sight and poised to spring?

Yokashima set his cup on the table next to his chair. "It is an interesting fact that people have committed an astounding variety of crimes to ensure the availability of tea. And yet, it is such an insipid drink. I shudder to think what they might do—what *I* might do—to protect the supply of coffee."

Was Yokashima speaking in metaphors or was he making idle conversation?

What a stupid question!

Yokashima wasn't the sort of man who made idle conversation.

That left *coffee* as a metaphor.

A metaphor for what?

There wasn't time to puzzle it out.

"Yes, Sensei," Vlod said. It seemed the safest response.

Yokashima picked up his mug, took a swallow of coffee, and returned the mug to its place on the table. "The Academy will be exceptionally dangerous for you."

Yokashima took another swallow. This time he did not return the mug to the table, but cupped his hands around it, as though its heat comforted him. His fingers were long and thin, like eagle's claws.

He added, "Today's attack proves as much."

"Yes, Sensei." It was time for one of Wolfram's frontal attacks. "Was it any of your doing?"

Rather than insulted, Yokashima looked as though Vlod's question had encouraged him, given him some scant cause for hope. "No, it was none of mine." He made a gesture that was neither apologetic nor resigned. "Sadly, the Academy is shot through with Thora's spies." He smiled. "With spies in general." The smile broadened. "Every one of our students is a spy, carrying tales, reporting information. Students love to show off."

There was no other way for it to be, Vlod thought. A student's bragging was his chieftain's invaluable information.

"The Academy is also overflowing with those who will seek to do you harm for their own reasons."

"I'm a target no matter where I am, Sensei," Vlod said.

"Don't be flippant."

"Perhaps it's a flippant truth."

"Do you genuinely wish to enroll?"

"Yes, Sensei."

Yokashima sipped his coffee. "You are a duelist, but Thora is an assassin. It will be my job to transform you into an assassin. It will be your job to keep yourself alive while I do mine."

"I understand, Sensei."

"No, you don't, but never mind," Yokashima said. He smiled a relaxed, resigned smile. "Thora loves power almost as I love coffee. I doubt you'll survive your first year."

"As much as that?"

Yokashima refilled their coffees. "I hope for your sake that you find whatever it is you are seeking."

TEN

er eminence, the Most Reverend Shabnan, Crone of the Cathedral Henge of Eileen the Immortal, breezed past the guards in the corridor, through the door, and into Thora's private sitting room.

With the debatable exceptions of the Blue Solarium and the Terrace Room, the sitting room was the airiest chamber in the whole of the Saraswati Palace, the Mother Metropolitan's residence. Quarried-glass windows graced two of the walls, the ceilings were high without attempting to intimidate, and the colors were off-whites with tan accents.

A low fire was burning on the hearth. It warded off the pre-fall chill, a chill that had begun, too early this year, to insinuate itself into the afternoons and evenings.

Unusually, Thora was alone, seated at her worktable, her secretary out of the room.

Shabnan closed the door and pointedly threw the bolt.

The place smelled of furniture polish and, more subtly, Thora's perfume.

It was a new scent, a gift from Narmer, one of the upriver chieftains. He was a crazed Egyptophile and overly ambitious, but he looked after his clan. And, Shabnan had to admit, he might prove useful as a counterbalance, if nothing else, to the likes of Edmund, the chieftain of Clan Iredale, or as an outright threat to Seldon, the chieftain of Clan Sauvie, holder of the infamous Manor Island.

But those were matters for another day.

Today's business was tiring enough.

There was hope, however, just weeks away.

Once the Mabon celebrations were behind them, once everyone had gone home, the Province of the Inland Empire and the Holy Oregon and, more specifically, the Cathedral Henge of Eileen the Immortal would be able to nestle down for the winter.

The roads and the rivers would become difficult, often impossible, to use, and because of it, Samhain and Yule would be intimate affairs, rather than large, public celebrations. There would be time for slow, relaxed dinners, not banquets, and long evenings before the fire, not endless rounds of extravagant entertaining. There would be time to read, to write, to dance, to sing, to pray, and, perhaps, to take a lover.

Winter was such a splendid season!

It was not, however, winter just yet, and before it arrived, sheltering them, there were issues to be discussed and settled.

Thora had a small blizzard of papers in front of her, a lamp, not burning, off to her left, a pen in her right hand, and a heavy shawl around her shoulders. A cup of tea, a teapot, an inkwell, and a blotter stood nearby.

Thora looked up from her work. "What is it?"

Her face was puffy, her complexion was pale and mottled, and her eyes had a tone about them that was both exhausted and frightened. The pregnancy was not going well. She was gaining far too much weight, and—face it—worst of all, she was visibly growing older.

"I hate to disturb you, Vladika, but we've received a missive from our man in Edmund's court."

"Something urgent?" Thora gestured toward the papers. "I hope."

Shabnan lay a sheet of paper on the table. "Bad news. The assassin failed."

Thora made a face. "Damn!"

"Indeed."

"Still, no surprise there. That boy leads a charmed life." She scanned the sheet. "No matter. Arrange a proper greeting for him at the Academy. We have people there. At least one or two of them ought to be skillful enough."

"Yes, Vladika. I'll send a courier immediately," Shabnan said.

"I want them to take their time. Nothing slapdash. Set him up and take him down."

"How many attempts will this make?"

Thora arched an eyebrow. "He'll be isolated there."

Shabnan shrugged. She'd heard such optimism before. "You're obsessed."

"No, I'm diligent, and he's as much of a threat as his father was."

"Why?" Shabnan asked. The Mother Metropolitan's obsession puzzled her. It was not irrational, but neither was it immediately explicable. Shivananda was dead. One would have thought that it was time to leave the scab alone. "What makes that boy so dangerous? Are you afraid he'll come seeking revenge?" She'd asked the question countless times, each time hoping that Thora would voice a different conclusion, each time knowing that she would not.

"Revenge has nothing to do with it," Thora said, a new steel, a new power in her voice. "Vlod is his father's son."

Eleven

Thora, Shabnan, Jinhai, and a few others had come out for elk.

They and the trackers had brought their heavy bows, and two of the men-at-arms accompanying the party had brought their compound crossbows.

The elk hadn't brought much of anything: acute senses, quick reflexes, four legs, four hooves, and horns; but the elk weren't the only creatures out and about.

Recently, the number of elk and deer had declined, while the number of wolves and tigers had increased. Thus, in order to balance the books, Thora and her party also intended to take any wolves, tigers, or mountain lions they encountered. The wolves were a genuine possibility, a tiger less so, while coming across a mountain lion this far away from the foothills would be an anomaly. Coyotes and feral dogs were also possibilities.

What Thora and her party came across was Master Yokashima.

He had positioned himself out in the open, out ahead of them, and had waited patiently for them to find him.

It was, Thora considered, a tactic that cut down on the number of embarrassed explanations on her part and on the number of the dead among her retinue.

Yokashima was mounted on a splendid chestnut, the sort of horse bred for speed and stamina. The master had a bow in a saddle scabbard and was wearing his two swords, one long and one short. From a distance it was impossible to tell how many other weapons he had. Most, she knew, were mere distractions.

Thora and her party reined in.

The smell of horses, leather, and warm clothing coiled around them.

One of Thora's men-at-arms made to ready her crossbow, but Shabnan, the Crone of the Cathedral, told her to, "Put that away before you get us all killed."

Yokashima remained where he was, unmoving.

Thora waved to him and nudged her horse forward.

Yokashima waited for her to come to him. He was like an oak, strong, defiant, and enduring. He was like a willow, supple and swaying with the winds. The storms never uprooted him because he permitted the winds to pass through him. He was eternal, and yet, he did not exist.

She reined in a comfortable distance away from him and waited. It was for him to approach and greet her.

He did neither. Instead, he spurred his horse and rode off to the west.

Thora watched him, growing smaller and smaller, disappearing into the trees.

With any luck a tiger would make a meal of him.

TWELVE

The normal course of study for a student at the Academy of Archmagus Basil the Anchorite and Wonderworker required four years to complete.

In the fall of Vlod's freshman year, between the Feast of Mabon and the first hard freeze, in the nineteenth year of her reign, Mother Metropolitan Thora miscarried in the fifth month of her pregnancy.

Acting at night and in secret, Thora and two members of her inner circle, women who were companions and confidants, not lickspittles, wrapped the fetus, a boy, in newly woven white linen and bound him round with strips of brown leather.

They carried him into the Sacred Grove, to a place that was not among the graves of the favored and honored few, nor among the graves of the previous mothers metropolitan and the crones of the cathedral, but in a separate section, private and apart. Here, ancient oaks would watch over him.

They had shed their leaves weeks ago, and their branches looked like raptor claws against the starry sky, a rarity for the time of year.

Thora dug the grave herself. She worked with a gardener's spading shovel. Decades of use had worn the handle smooth and given it a glossy patina. The blade was sharp, and it cut smoothly through the soil.

Thora lifted the black earth from the ground, drinking in the rich perfume of it. She set the soil aside, making of it a neat mound beside the opening.

When she was satisfied that she had dug down far enough, she drove the blade of the shovel deep into the mound and knelt beside the yawning hole.

The ground was muddy and soaked through her skirts, chilling her knees.

She held out her hands, and Shabnan, the Cathedral's Crone and Thora's sometime lover, passed Thora the white-wrapped bundle. Shabnan was in her very late forties. She was a handsome woman, with the lean build and quick reflexes of a huntress.

She rarely gave way to tears, but tonight her eyes were damp, her complexion blotchy, her movements without grace. She despised death, especially the death of a child. The whole notion of it offended her, not because she was squeamish but because death contradicted her faith in the divine.

This attitude was, of course, the old, old trap, and she recognized it for what it was. Nevertheless, she could not free herself from it. No, the best she could do was to acknowledge it, while also doing her best to ignore it.

Thora cradled the bundle against her chest. He felt cold and dead and unmoving. No great surprise there. He *was* cold and dead and unmoving.

Above all else, he felt *absent*.

But it was his tiny size and his utter lack of weight that threatened to unnerve her. They tightened her throat and blurred her vision and caused her hands to tremble.

Had she never seen death before?

She had, times without number, but it had yet to grow familiar. It had yet to become tolerable. She was like Shabnan in that.

Thora's thoughts circled back.

Even though she had prepared and dressed and wrapped him herself, she had expected him to be heavier. How was it that he weighed next to nothing?

There was more to it than his tiny size.

And that absence.

What of that?

She reined in.

Enough of this. Indeed too much. She must move on. Move on. Move on. Move on. The Wheel is never still. And her time was growing short. She was nearer to the end than to the beginning.

She had no right to cling, and it would be her undoing if she tried.

Fall follows summer, and winter follows fall.

It is the eternal turning of the Wheel.

Move on!

Move on!

Make haste!

Thora lay the boy in his grave. She took a priest's amulet from a pocket and laid it on the child's chest. Only the ordained could rest in the Grove, and with the presentation of the amulet, she ordained him.

No, it wasn't in strict accordance with the canons, and, yes, her motives were sentimental rather than theological, but she seriously doubted that if anyone ever learned of what she had done, that they would take offense, much less dare to complain.

She had acted within her rights. She had acted *in extremis*, and there was an end to it. If someone did object, then so much the worse for them.

Ulricka, Thora's current favorite, and something, perhaps, of a true confidant, despite her youth, handed Thora the shovel.

Thora scooped up a shovelful of earth from the mound.

To the child, Thora said, "May the Gods and the Generations protect your journey. Return to us in health!"

"So and blessed let it be!" Shabnan and Ulricka chorused.

The Crone's voice had eased into the lowering tones of middle age, but Ulricka's voice rang bright and clear. She was twenty-one, but her voice was that of a woman with her Virgin's Year a mere season or two behind her. It was not the voice of a child, but neither was it the voice of a matron with a husband and a gaggle of runny-nosed offspring.

Ulricka's life at the Cathedral had helped. A Child of the Cathedral, born to a girl completing her Virgin's Year, Ulricka had had the good fortune to be raised at the Cathedral, rather than be assigned to one of the clans.

After completing her own Virgin's Year, she had been permitted to stay on at the Cathedral. She had graduated from the seminary and was ordained, but then, rather than take an active part in the priesthood, she had gone into the grinding, pinching world of administration.

Being able to bridge between the hierarchy and the bureaucracy, and being able to tell the difference, she had made herself unusually useful in Thora's court.

In truth, the Wheel is never still.

Thora dropped the first shovelful of earth onto the bundle.

Setting the shovel aside, casting it away as though it were a hateful thing, she dropped to her knees and carefully packed handful after handful of earth around her miscarried son, as though she were tucking him in for the night.

The earth was dark and moist and grainy, not a bit like sand, nor a bit like clay. It was perfect for farming, for gardening. It was the product of century upon century of devout tending.

She had no idea why she packed the dirt around him so carefully, but it seemed to be the appropriate thing, to be his due.

She took solace from the act, from the spontaneous ritual.

Those who tended the Sacred Grove, who weeded it, who turned the earth, who pruned the trees, who hauled away the fallen limbs, who spaded in the fallen leaves, who turned in the ash and the dung, who trimmed around the headstones, who cut the lawns—those were, she thought, the happiest people at the Cathedral.

She had never been able to understand their contentment before, their special piety, but now, working the dirt in around what might have been another of her sons, she glimpsed the truth of their lives.

She packed in the last handful of dirt and wiped her hands on her skits, leaving behind muddy smears.

Oranges, she thought.

Oranges?

Why had she thought of oranges? Never mind. She had.

And because she had, she decided that she must build a special greenhouse and plant orange trees in it, if she could find the seedlings, or raise them from the seeds of the oranges she had.

Surely, in one way or another, it must be possible. She could have seedlings sent up from the San Joaquin, if nothing else. Mother Metropolitan Rhea was a treasure when it came to such things. Thora could send her smoked salmon in return.

She stood.

She would have to find the glass, too. The quarry sites had been stripped long, long ago, but supplies of plate glass had to exist somewhere. And if they didn't, perhaps it would be possible to manufacture new glass of sufficient quality and in sufficient quantities.

She brushed off her skirts.

It was done.

From start to finish, she had not cried, she had not collapsed, she had not turned away, and her voice had not broken.

The thought of it calmed her.

She would need that strength in the months to come, unless she was very, very wrong.

As they were walking out of the Sacred Grove, with the wind soughing in the higher branches of the trees and the ground soft but not sodden beneath their booted feet, Thora said, "I shall build a greenhouse."

"Of what sort, Vladika?" Ulricka asked.

"Tall. Very large. Heated. With beehives."

"Ah, a veritable Crystal Palace," Shabnan said. "The glaziers will adore you, Vladika."

"What will you grow in it?" Ulricka asked.

"Oranges," Thora said. "I shall grow oranges."

A few days later, a package about the size of a folded blanket arrived for Thora. It was neatly bound in new canvas. Yokashima had sent it.

Thora dismissed the servant who had laid it on the catch-all table in Thora's sitting room.

A fire was burning on the hearth, and the chamber had a cozy feel to it, although Thora felt anything but cozy.

The package's presence didn't help.

"You ought to open it," Shabnan said.

Without responding directly, Thora dismissed Ulricka and the three or four others she'd been meeting with, everyone but Shabnan.

The door closed, the latch clicked, and Thora and the Crone stared down at the bundle.

"Rattlesnakes?" Shabnan asked.

"No buzzing."

"Scorpions, then."

"Too large," Thora said.

"Large scorpions."

"A short sword and instructions on how to commit seppuku?" Thora asked, playing along.

"Wrong shape."

"He included the ceremonial garb and a mat?"

"How considerate of him," Shabnan said. "He is such a polite fellow, don't you think?"

They stared at the bundle.

"There's nothing for it, I suppose," Thora said, and untied the heavy cords.

The wrapping came away in a flutter of the aroma of new canvas. Even to Thora, it was a heady scent, one that spoke of sails and ships and crossing mighty oceans.

Revealed was a tiger skin.

It had been so recently treated that it still gave off the aroma of the processes, although not strongly. The head was snarling, as tradition dictated, and the glass eyes gazed out, hauntingly expressive.

Expressive, yes, and then some, but of what?

No matter, the tiger skin was an extravagant gift.

Just then a note fluttered to the floor.

Thora scooped it up and read it.

"Well, what does our murderous little friend have to say?" Shabnan asked.

"Not what I'd expected," Thora said.

Your Beatitude,

The previous owner introduced himself in such an aggressive manner that I felt obliged to relieve him of his earthly burdens.

When you gaze at this souvenir, remember that I understand more than you might imagine I do.

Your servant,

Yokashima

"*Understand* what?" Shabnan asked. "What *more*?"

For a woman who could think circles around the best minds at the Cathedral, Shabnan could be as dense as a block of granite.

"Yokashima hasn't always been a martial-arts instructor," Thora said. "There are stories, rumors, of a rebellion gone terribly wrong and of a family who paid the price."

"Then why isn't he dead?" Shabnan said. "I thought that was their way."

"Most of the time," Thora said. "Remember, Yokashima is not most people."

"No, he most certainly is not."

Thora looked down on the skin. She stroked the head between the eyes, as though the tiger might enjoy that. "Have this fellow hung on my bedroom wall, will you?"

Thirteen

By this time, the Academy of Archmagus Basil the Anchorite and Wonderworker had overcome the chaos of launching a new academic year, as it always did, and it had come through the Feast of Mabon as well as anyone could expect, as it usually did.

The former was due to the excitement of a new academic year. The latter was due to the Academy's practice of limiting its observation of Mabon to the single day of the autumnal equinox.

The Academy's brief local celebration was in direct contrast to the weeklong, province-wide festivals held at the Cathedral Henge of Eileen the Immortal.

With Mabon behind it, and with virtually everyone able to find the correct lecture hall at the correct time, the Academy had settled into its rhythm.

One evening, well into the term, after Vlod had finished eating in the Palmer Hall refectory, he trudged up to the room he shared with Aerian. Aerian was a junior who reminded Vlod of an excitable wolfhound. He had a long, thin face, a long nose, and long, large teeth.

Everything about him was long, except his fingers, which were on the stubby side.

He blamed his fingers on his maternal grandmother and credited his father for the rest of his stature. His father, Aerian claimed, looked like a tall, anorexic heron.

As far as Vlod was concerned, being assigned a junior for a roommate had been a stroke of first-day luck, but that bit of good fortune hadn't happened along until after Vlod had come perilously close to killing someone.

As instructed, two weeks before the autumnal equinox, Vlod had arrived at the Academy of Archmagus Basil the Anchorite and Wonderworker. Rather, he arrived at the approach to the main gatehouse, a massive, glowering structure. It was, however, covered, somewhat paradoxically for a fortification, with ivy.

The Academy stood at the head of an enormous cleared area on the western slope of Mt. Hood. The area was a patchwork of pastures, orchards, vegetable gardens, and greenhouses.

Given the geography, the Academy's position was militarily unassailable. Admittedly, an enemy could lay siege to the Academy itself, but as soon as winter had taken hold, the rain, sleet, snow, ice, and the unrelenting winds would force its abandonment.

Over the centuries, people who were as naïve as they were desperate had attempted various assaults and sieges, but none had succeeded.

These days, one of the diverting things that happened during the spring planting season was the discovery of discarded weapons. Generally, these proved to be the relics of one or another of those failed attempts. Or they turned out to be the detritus of a failed robbery, a failed intelligence-gathering mission, or a failed assassination.

It was often said that it was one such find that had sparked Shivananda's love for archeology, or, as some liked to phrase it, his obsession with digging through other people's garbage.

Physically, the Academy consisted of a cluster of granite-and-timber buildings, some as many as five stories tall, many adorned with towers.

Rock-and-granite curtain walls, inner and outer, complete with hoardings and throwing engines, surrounded the main complex.

Flags and streamers flew from the towers, and banners hung down from the crenellations. Only the main gatehouse had been left bereft of bunting.

Vlod reigned in his horse and stared in appreciation at the massive structure. It was a third-again as high as the outer curtain wall and consisted of two massive, linked towers, with the doors and portcullis nestled in between. The towers and their connecting wall were crenelated, and the merlons were fitted with arrow loops. No hoardings.

The portcullis had been raised and the doors stood open, but despite the appearance of welcome, uniformed archers patrolled the battlements, and men-at-arms guarded the gate.

A small, three-sided tent stood before the gatehouse. A sign over its entrance flap announced, "Registrar."

A short line of students had formed. Some were goggling at their surroundings, while others were affecting to be bored silly. Each had his duffle and saddle bags with him.

Vlod tethered his horse and joined the line.

Soon enough, he was standing in front of a makeshift trestle table. Two people were seated behind it. One was older, and the other much, much younger. Vlod took the older to be the registrar or a registrar's clerk, and the younger, who had to be his assistant, had the impatient, sneering look of someone who could only be an upperclassman.

Off to one side was a second table. It had been carelessly littered with confiscated items, each tagged. Among them were various bottles, jars, and vials; small boxes; small daggers; sets of shuriken; books of pornography; two obvious grimoires; a book whose cover announced that it was the *I Ching* but which probably wasn't; and a highly polished stick about twice the length of a man's foot.

The clerk smiled. "Your name, please." He was small and had a thin, questing face. He looked, Vlod thought, like a ferret. His voice, however, was surprisingly deep.

"Vlod of the Iredales," Vlod said.

The clerk scanned down a list. "Ah, here you are. Good. Glad you could make it. Any trouble on the roads?"

"No, sir."

The assistant made a tick mark on a list of his own.

The clerk said, "May I have your letter of admission, your chieftain's certificate of permission to attend, and your proof of financial resources?"

Vlod handed across the documents.

His palms tingled. Would they actually let him in, or would they send him away? They might do either. After all, his father's heresy had been no small matter.

The clerk glanced through the documents. "Everything appears to be in order," he said.

That was a relief. The clerk could have rejected them out of hand, no genuine reason required. A hunch would do.

The clerk made a few notes and returned the papers to Vlod.

The assistant was another story. His arrogance was as thick on the ground as mud after a gale. He was hunting for an excuse, hoping for one to appear.

After a long moment, the registrar's clerk said, "Vlod. Of the Iredales. I was one of your father's friends." He looked as though he were about to add something, but didn't.

And what, Vlod wondered, had this self-proclaimed friend been doing while Vlod's father was being murdered? Had he spoken out at the trial, or had he kept silent?

The clerk said, "I'll have to inspect your things. Regulations, you understand."

Both Wolfram and Yokashima had warned Vlod about this part of the procedure—the search for contraband. Vlod handed over his duffle bag.

"Your saddlebags, too," the clerk's student assistant snapped, surly, combative.

Vlod's anger flared, but he checked it. "Oh, sorry," he said, feigning surprise, and put them on the table next to his duffle.

Initially, going through the duffle, the registrar's clerk turned up nothing of interest. No crib notes, no untoward amounts of cash, no forbidden drugs, no poisons, no unauthorized reference materials, no supposedly magic wands.

Then the clerk turned to the saddlebags. He rummaged through them and drew out a book.

Before and After the Second Creation, Transcending the Physical

Senses by Ulysses Slocum.

His face lighted. "Oh, I remember this book. It was your father's favorite. I assume you've read it."

"Several times," Vlod said.

"What a marvel this little volume is," the clerk said. "Just imagine it!" He gestured with the book, gently, as though it might shatter. "This is one of the very last books to be printed by machine. Moveable type! Bound by hand, though. All that stitching, all that glue." He very carefully opened the book. "The printing is so very, very clear, even after all these centuries. Obviously, acid-free paper. What a treasure!"

"Wasn't it declared a heretical work?" the assistant asked.

"By the *Cathedral*, yes, but not by us. Really, Grady, you must learn to welcome the challenging."

The clerk returned the book to its place, rummaged a little more, and pulled out a leather-wrapped volume. It was about twice the size of a man's hand. "Another book?" he asked. His eyes were sparkling.

"It's very fragile," Vlod said. "I shouldn't have brought it, but I couldn't leave it behind."

The clerk undid the wrapping.

Revealed was a battered volume. The spine was gone and the front and back covers were cracked as though they were about to disintegrate.

"How old?" the clerk asked.

"It survived the Great Winter. The pages that would date it have been lost."

"Not by you?"

"No, nor by my father," Vlod said. "It was another of his, well, his books."

"His library was confiscated, wasn't it?"

"The two I have were overlooked."

"Hidden, more likely," Grady said.

Ignoring his assistant, the clerk read the title: "*Speculations on the Future of Civilization, the Coming Prohibition of Rational Thought* by Master Bob." He looked at the fragile pages as though they might burn him. "I'm not familiar with Master Bob. Who was he?"

"I'm not sure," Vlod said. "I believe he was a teacher and mystic, a swami, if you will. He's believed to have lived on what are now Iredale lands."

"Our library has a handwritten copy of this book," the clerk said. "Our librarian would be most grateful were you to lend this one to him so he can correct our copy."

"It would be my pleasure."

The clerk closed the book, rewrapped it, and returned it to the saddle bag. "Take special care of those two."

"Yes, sir."

"Don't misunderstand, but with volumes like those in his possession, it's no wonder they made up an excuse to burn your father. Shivananda was very brave, and a good friend, but he was a touch careless."

Vlod's emotions flared again, and again he checked them. The registrar's clerk hadn't meant his remarks to be unkind or abrasive. He had meant them merely as observations.

But couldn't he have also meant them as a warning? Or possibly as a threat? No, not as threat.

"I keep them as reminders of him," Vlod said, "and for their own value."

The assistant said, "If they'd burned my father at the stake for heresy, I'd do my best to forget him."

"Grady!" the clerk said.

But the rebuke came too late.

In less time than it had taken the clerk to speak, Vlod drew and pressed the edge of his sword into the soft flesh at the base of the assistant's throat.

Those in line behind Vlod scrambled to get clear.

A long, tense silence took over the tent, and passersby stopped to look, to stare into the shadowed space.

Neither Vlod, nor the registrar's clerk, nor Grady moved or spoke.

The rush and trickle of Grady's bladder giving way broke the silence.

The clerk's embarrassed laugh rippled through the tent, and a look of absolute shame took over Grady's face, but neither Vlod's attention nor his sword wavered in the slightest.

"You know," the clerk said, affably, "I haven't seen that stroke in many, many years. They tell me it's quite popular among the downriver clans."

"It has it uses," Vlod said. He rocked the blade, causing a slight flow of blood. It trickled down Grady's neck and down the blade of Vlod's sword toward the hilt. "It serves to warn, rather than to kill."

"Indeed, it does," the clerk said. "Toleration is such a splendid virtue."

"We Iredale's are a tolerant bunch," Vlod said. "We do not take revenge on animals and fools."

"Rightly so," the registrar's clerk said.

Vlod flicked his sword clear of Grady's neck, wiped the blood from the steel, and re-sheathed the blade.

The clerk told Grady to have his wound seen to, and the upperclassman bolted from the tent.

"You've made an enemy, there," the clerk said.

"It would have been worse if I'd let him get away with it."

"Away with what? Making a gauche remark?"

"With deliberately insulting my father."

"You give him too much credit."

"I overreacted?"

"Time will tell," the clerk said. "Time will tell."

He handed Vlod a packet of papers. "Your registration materials. Classes begin tomorrow at eight. Be prompt. Don't dawdle. About your room assignment. I've put you in with Aerian. He's one of our few level-headed juniors. Palmer Hall, room 305."

"Thank you."

"No need, no need," the clerk said. "But, please, as a favor to me, don't decapitate more than one or two of your fellow students."

Palmer Hall was a stone-and-timber edifice, tucked in between the Academy's keep and its inner curtain wall. It was high on the upland side of the complex. Its two distinct features were its steeply peaked roof —to bear the weight of the winter snows—and a wide, covered front porch—to provide a modicum of protection from the rain.

Two students lounged on the steps. The one on Vlod's left had blond hair, while the one on his right had been graced with oily brown hair and an overabundance of pimples. Their smug superiority marked them as upperclassmen.

The twin facts that they were lounging on the steps and that they were the only ones lounging on the steps announced their intention to pick a fight.

Evidently, Grady had friends.

Vlod resettled his saddlebags across his left shoulder. The buckles were fastened, and his father's books laid heavily against his chest. Satisfied that everything was as secure as could be, he continued on toward the building.

Blondie hooked a thumb off to one side. "Freshmen use the back door."

So it was going to be that sort of an encounter…

"Thank you. I'll try to remember," Vlod said, and started toward the side of the building.

The back door had to be around in the back, didn't it? There was a curtain wall back there, but there had to be a door, too, didn't there? They'd just told him so, hadn't they?

Vlod heard the crunch of a boot on the path behind him and swung around.

Blondie and Pimples were advancing toward him, strutting, separating, sneering at him.

They were opening their attack.

"We didn't give you permission to leave," Pimples said.

"I didn't understand I needed any," Vlod said. "Please accept my apologies."

"Not good enough, runt," Blondie said.

"I'm sorry if my apology appears inadequate." Vlod wondered if either of them understood half of what he had just said. "Please excuse me."

"Not a chance," Pimples said.

Blondie closed in. "Grady told us about what happened."

So Vlod had been right. These two were a couple of Grady's stooges. How many did he have? More than two, certainly.

"Then you know he was out of line," Vlod said.

"Let's see the books, runt."

"I'm not a library," Vlod said.

"You are if we say you are," Pimples said.

"Yeah, hand 'em over," Blondie said, raising his voice.

Was there nothing new under the sun?

Even that adolescent complaint was hackneyed.

Vlod set his duffle down on the path. "No."

Blondie rushed in and made a grab for the saddlebags, but Vlod pivoted away and kicked him in the stomach, driving in the heel of his boot. He added a sharp twist for good measure.

With an open-mouthed grunt, Blondie doubled over and dropped to his knees.

Pimples rushed.

Vlod threw a backfist to his temple.

Pimples staggered across the lawn.

More or less recovered, Blondie lunged, as though he intended to seize Vlod's legs; but Vlod rebalanced his stance and kicked, landing the heel of his boot on his assailant's cheek bone, close to his nose but not directly on it.

To have struck Blondie's nose squarely would have driven the inevitable bone splinters up into the brain, killing the poor oversized ninny, assuming of course that he had a brain. Nevertheless, the blow had landed close enough and at just the right angle to give Blondie a gushing nosebleed.

Blondie was on the ground again. In addition to the nosebleed, the skin over his cheekbone was turning a bright red. A wretched bruise was bound to form.

"You son of a bitch!" Blondie shouted, and started to get up. "You fucking coward!"

The words shot back and forth along the curtain wall, along the wall of the residence hall.

Vlod planted a foot at the base of Blondie's throat, forcing him down onto the grass beside the path. "Be still! You offend the tranquility of the afternoon."

Blondie wasn't the only one offending the tranquility of the afternoon. Pimples had shaken off Vlod's blow to his temple and was circling around to attack Vlod from behind.

Without reversing his stance, Vlod drew his sword and held it out to his side, at a downward angle. The steel flashed in the sunlight and the aroma of whale oil added a subtle note to the scene.

Pimples stopped in midstride.

"Good choice," Vlod said.

Vlod moved away from Blondie and brought both of them into view. Pimples was a scant two paces away, much closer than Vlod had judged him to be. It was a surprising miscalculation and one that might have cost him his life under different circumstances.

Brenna would have laughed at him, but Wolfram, had he witnessed such an error, would have made his displeasure known...and felt, like as not. How many times had the Iredale's battlemaster cuffed home an important lesson? Vlod could count them on the fingers of one hand, but each lesson had become indelible.

Blondie levered himself to his feet. "This isn't over."

"Fuck, it hasn't even started," Pimples chimed in, an eager smirk on his face.

"I'm at your disposal," Vlod said, and backed away in the direction of his duffel bag.

Suddenly, a three-fingered grip seized the wrist of his sword arm, opening the hand as easily as one might open a cupboard door. A brown hand caught his sword before it touched the ground and took it away.

Vlod struck at his new, unseen assailant, but he finished on the ground, staring up into a decidedly Asian face, a Japanese face, a face that Vlod recognized. He felt, however, as though he were seeing it for the first time. The features spoke of middle-age and of an old, burdensome grief, but the eyes, which were clear and dark beyond description, sang of the ages and heroes of a distant and forbidden past.

No small amount of awe seized Vlod. It penetrated his very being, and it held him as tightly as those three iron fingers had.

"Royce," Master Yokashima said, "take Mueller to the infirmary. His nose may be broken."

"Yes, Sensei!" Pimples said, bowing rapidly. The gesture was closer to a head bob than a true bow, a relaxed formality.

When Mueller (the blond one) and Royce (the pimpled one) had gone, Yokashima looked down at Vlod.

"Get up, you little fool."

Vlod got up and stood silently. It seemed the safest thing to do, the best way to avoid causing further anger. No, that wasn't the right word. The correct word was *disappointment*.

Why? What had Vlod done? What had he failed to do?

"Are Grady and those two in Thora's stable?" Vlod asked.

"They are upperclassmen."

Which didn't entirely answer the question.

"By the way, your technique was terrible," Yokashima said. "Where was the boy I fought with? Where was the boy who so expertly dropped his would-be assassin?"

Vlod didn't dare to answer.

"It must be the altitude," Yokashima said. "I can think of no other explanation." A long, painful silence. "You misjudged Royce's position, and thus you drew blindly."

"Yes, Sensei."

With real force, quiet though it was, Yokashima said, "Worst of all, you were *showing off*." He slapped Vlod across the face, not a hard blow but strong enough to underline the point. Wolfram would have applauded. "You shame your teachers. You shame your clan. You shame yourself! You shame *me*!"

Shades of that encounter with Morven all those years ago—the student's pride shaming his teachers. Vlod could almost hear Wolfram's voice saying Master Yokashima's words.

But Yokashima's ego, whatever loss of face Vlod may have caused him, had nothing to do with it. Of that Vlod had no doubt. Yokashima's reputation, then? His position as the Academy's master of the martial arts?

Vlod bowed. "I acted without thinking. I humbly apologize."

A second blow, harder than the first, intended to punish as well as emphasize. "No excuses! And no apologies!"

Who was this man, the man behind the reputation, the position, the skill? What was his game? Whatever Yokashima's game was, Vlod promised himself not to be afraid of him, not as Royce and Mueller plainly were. "Yes, Sensei!"

"Humility paves the path of the true warrior."

Yokashima looked as though he had more to say, but whatever it was, he was leaving it for another time.

"Yes, Sensei!" Vlod said.

Yokashima sighted along the edge of Vlod's blade. "This weapon has seen battle. Several times."

A touch of pride wove its way between the weaving strands of Vlod's awe and his simultaneous anger, but that pride was an even greater danger than any sort of cowardice ever could be. Cowardice could lose battles, but pride could lose whole clans, whole peoples. And, too, it led to showing off. "Yes, Sensei."

But humility? How did the humble man gather the resolve to defeat an opponent? How did the humble man keep himself alive? What was Vlod missing?

Yokashima was saying, "It is a newer blade. Was it forged for you?"

"Yes, Sensei."

Yokashima returned Vlod's sword. "The registrar—yes, he was the registrar, not a clerk, as you might have assumed. He asked you to limit yourself to one or two decapitations, did he not?" A brief smile at the humor that had encased the registrar's warning. "I am *telling* you not to complicate my task by playing children's games. If heads are to fly, I shall be the one to launch them, not you, and I shall do it as inconspicuously as possible."

And with that, Vlod was waved away as though he were a bothersome insect.

Room 305 turned out to be a suite equipped with a bathroom and a cooking hearth; while Aerian, the level-headed junior, turned out to have no desire to bully anyone, let alone a sword-wielding freshman from a clan that bred warriors like a bog breeds mosquitos.

"I saw your encounter with Yoki-Shoki," Aerian said.

"Who?"

"The sensei. Master Yokashima. He's a good teacher, none better, but he's rough. Loves riddles. Delights in knocking his students around." Aerian gave Vlod an appraising look, as though he were trying to decide which way to bet. He shrugged as those reaching an unexpected conclusion do, and said, "I'm told you're the heretic's kid."

The second time in less than an hour. The whole Academy must know. Which, of course, they did. There had never been the slightest chance they wouldn't. "That's what I'm told."

Another appraising look. "I've heard at least as many rumors about you as there are crows on a garbage pile." Aerian smiled in one corner of his mouth. "All right, spill it," he said. "What did he do?"

"My father? I'm not sure. The gist of it is that he suggested the Second Creation ought to be treated as pious myth rather than as historical fact."

"Shit," Aerian said. "No wonder they burned him."

Despite himself, Vlod chuckled. It was a release of sorts. "You're the second person who's told me that today."

"Sorry."

"Don't be."

The embarrassment left Aerian's face. "Then what were Mueller and Royce after? Petty harassment?"

"A couple of old books." Vlod's attitude relaxed a notch further. "They belonged to my father. Now they're mine. I made the mistake of bringing them with me."

"What'll Mueller do with them?"

"Not Mueller, a fellow named Grady."

"Grady? That piece of shit? I ought to ask you to room with somebody else. What does he want with them?"

"I'm the heretic's kid, remember?"

"Thanks for reminding me," Aerian said. "It had nearly slipped my mind."

"Do you want me to find another room?"

"Hell, no. Any enemy of Grady's is a friend of mine."

Now, with that welcome to the Academy weeks in the past, Vlod opened the door to room 305 and started through. He was looking forward to a decent cup of coffee and, with much less anticipation, to a long, quiet night with his studies.

The first round of midterms was coming up, and like everyone else, he was already behind. Each of their instructors was piling on the work as if each class were the *only* class that any of their students were taking.

However, Vlod was benefiting from a stroke of luck. Grady, Mueller, and Royce were keeping to themselves.

On the not-so-lucky side, Master Yokashima was running Vlod's class through drill after drill. He often left them in horse stance for the entire period. Another favorite was to repeat the same kata, time after time, until their eyes, figuratively, crossed. When he was feeling particularly enthusiastic, he would lead them on cross-country runs, pushing them as no middle-aged man ought to have been able to.

"Before the rain gets going," he once said, grinning, in the midst of a frigid downpour.

Plus there were days spent in the fields and greenhouses, in the barns, in the storerooms, in the abattoirs, and in the kitchens. Foods and medicines didn't grow themselves, collect themselves, preserve themselves, or prepare themselves.

But Vlod was almost in his room now, almost free to stir up the fire, to make a pot of coffee, and to settle down to his current round of assignments. He was nearly free to let the quiet buoy him.

Suddenly, without the slightest warning, the door jerked open, and Vlod was pulled on into the room.

Vlod glimpsed his attacker: Royce!

FOURTEEN

Royce tripped Vlod. At the same time, Royce struck Vlod's back, hard, right between the shoulder blades. This combination of moves, the pull and the blow, propelled Vlod farther forward and down onto the floor. It was a brawler's tactic, but effective.

Two other figures rushed out of the shadows: Grady and Mueller.

Rather than curl into a defensive ball, Vlod rolled onto his back and sprang to his feet, readying himself to counterattack.

Grady kicked the door shut. "Did you think we'd forgotten about you?"

"I'd had my hopes," Vlod said.

"Not one fucking chance in hell," Grady said. "We never forget."

"That makes us even."

Mueller said, "We haven't forgotten about those books, either. As a matter of fact, that's why we've dropped by, to borrow them."

"What do you say, eh, runt?" Royce said. "Can we borrow your precious books or not?"

For the first time since the attack had begun, a pang of doubt gripped Vlod. He'd been caught in ambushes before, had faced worse odds before, but never before had he been unarmed. He had a knife in his boot and another up one sleeve—the registrar had missed that one—

but he had no way to draw either of them without giving them an ideal opportunity to attack.

"Answer me, runt!" Mueller demanded.

"The library is across the quad," Vlod said. his mouth had gone dry, and his hands had begun to sweat. His doubt was turning into fear. It was as though Wolfram and the Iredale's way-masters had taught him nothing.

Mueller pulled the two ancient books from the shelf on Vlod's side of the sitting room. "We don't need a library. We have you!"

"I'm warning you. Put those back!" It was a pathetic thing to say.

"Make me!" Mueller said.

Vlod attacked, but Grady and Royce countered. They writhed back and forth, but then Mueller came over, shoved into the melee, and punched Vlod in the face.

Vlod fell backward, his weight thrown against Grady and Royce.

Vlod thrashed wildly in an effort to escape, to gain room, but they held him fast.

Vlod cursed his lack of size, his lack of care, strolling through Palmer Hall and into his room as though he were safe, as though the threats Grady and the others had made had magically disappeared. He ought to have had better sense. He ought to have known that Grady wouldn't stop until Vlod had defeated him. It was the only way with bullies.

Royce popped the side of Vlod's head with an elbow strike. "Hold still!"

"Well, well," Grady said, "you are in a fix, aren't you?"

"I've been in worse," Vlod said.

"I doubt it," Mueller said.

Mueller handed the books to Grady, who held them up for Vlod to see.

"Pay close attention, runt," Grady said. "I'm not here to steal anything. I'll let you have these fuckers back when I'm done with them —if you behave yourself. Tell anyone I have them and I'll toss 'em onto the nearest fire. Understand?"

"Give them back!"

Grady drove his fist into the pit of Vlod's stomach. "Wail if I've made myself clear," he said, and repeated the strike, twisting his fist, grinding it into the viscera.

Vlod dropped onto all fours and threw up.

"Puking wasn't one of your choices," Grady said, "but considering how generous you've been, I'll accept it."

"Puking as a form of communication. Who'd have thought it?" Royce said.

He and Mueller jerked Vlod upright. The violent movement sent a shot of pain down into Vlod's pelvic floor and up into his throat. It surged on up and across his forehead. The pain reduced his vision to dark blurs.

"You know," Grady said, "around here getting beat up could become a way of life for you."

"Give them back," Vlod said. "I won't ask again."

Mueller said, "You got that right."

And then the true beating began. Stomach, head, ribs, face. Over and over, his face. Blood gushed from his nose. It flowed across his mouth and dribbled from his chin. Tears and snot streamed. His bladder and bowels cut loose, which only redoubled their rage, their delight.

On and on.

After a time, the blows failed to register as anything greater than dull thuds. They became as sounds, not as sensations.

The sounds stopped.

Silence.

The three of them had gone.

How long ago?

A few minutes? A few hours?

Vlod couldn't tell.

He was alone.

There was blood, urine, and feces smeared on the floor all around where he lay. The mixture had soaked into his tunic and had caked on his face and in his hair.

There was shame and humiliation, but there was also little pain.

He would have welcomed it as a distraction from the loss of his father's books.

Very little pain.

He tried to figure out whether that was a good sign or a bad one. It could be either, but what was it in this case? When all pain has fled, can death be far away? Even pain fears death.

Had they beaten him so badly that he was going to die?

He immediately let go of the question.

He couldn't answer it, and asking it served no purpose.

He crawled into the bathroom, hung his head over the rim of the toilet, and threw up...or tried to.

Once the retching, the dry retching, had subsided, he pulled himself up and leaned over the washstand.

At least his legs and feet worked. A good sign. Maybe they hadn't killed him.

Unless they'd ruptured his spleen or his gut or had caused a brain bleed. They might have. Then he'd either bleed to death or rot to death from the inside out or his brain would quit.

He checked for broken ribs. Miraculously, only one was questionable. The rest were sound. And his nose. They hadn't broken it. How was that possible? Were they saving it as a treat for another day?

He rinsed his mouth and splashed water on his face.

Fresh blood spattered down into the basin, but the flow was lessening.

He cleaned up as well as he could.

He put on clean clothes and set the soiled ones aside to launder.

Pressing a damp towel to his mouth and nose, he stumbled back into the sitting room and eased himself into a chair.

They had stolen his father's books.

The door opened. "What the hell?" It was Aerian. Three quick steps and he was standing over Vlod. "Who did this to you?"

"I can't say." Vlod smiled. "I tripped over my own ego."

The room took a violent lurch, and Vlod felt himself ebb away, not to die, but to slip down into the soft, cradling arms of unconsciousness.

FIFTEEN

A week after Vlod's beating, when it had become clear that he would heal rather than die, he dressed and went for a walk. It was his first excursion outside of Palmer Hall.

The late fall air was cold, the sort of cold that penetrated, that burrowed into the bone marrow.

With nowhere specific to go, Vlod wandered through the Academy.

Rather than providing an escape, its streets and alleys closed in upon him. Limping slightly, his face raw with bruises and scabbed-over splits, with one of his eyes swollen nearly shut, he drew a great number of stares, and of quizzical looks. His presence sparked a great many whispered questions and hurried explanations.

"Grady..."

"...over a book."

"I heard it was two books."

"He's the heretic's son..."

"Serves him right. He's an arrogant, little..."

"Did you hear what he did to Grady in the tent?"

"It's no wonder they..."

"...and the registrar let him get away with it, too."

"How does he rate?"

"Something had to be done. Well, didn't it?"

Vlod left the crowded places behind and climbed up to the top of the inner curtain wall, to the battlements.

His body repented of its recent sloth and fired him with the sensation that with each step, each breath, each time he gripped a railing, he was tearing his muscles and joints asunder.

He could feel the recently healed tissues popping open. The ache in his bruised bones was worse than the original blows.

Nausea boiled through his stomach, but it calmed down as soon as he reached the top of his climb and could look out, as soon as he could feel the breeze on his face.

He gazed at the fields and greenhouses surrounding the Academy, and then he turned and studied Mt. Hood and its newest fall of snow. The air was sharp and dry and smelled of snow and ice. The cold, as desiccated as the salt-bleached ocean drift of summer, caressed him, soothed him, and made him long for home, for gray coastal skies and for the howling, honest storms of winter.

And the gulls.

Apart from the people, he missed the great, white, wheeling gulls the most.

A gust of wind, right off the snowfields, billowed his cloak around his legs. Fall was merging into winter.

His father's books. He must recover them. But how?

No answer.

Defeated, Vlod resumed his walk.

This time, however, he had a destination in mind: a place in which to enter the Shaw Island Style, assuming he was healed enough to perform it.

Windswept and bitterly cold, the practice field was deserted.

He went to what passed for a sheltered corner and stood very still. He looked at a spot on the ground four meters ahead of him. He slowed his breathing.

He released the monkey chatter in his mind, and stepped into the eternal flow.

The Wild Horse Parts His Mane.

Utter failure.

He tried again to relax his muscles, to calm the monkeys.

The Wild Horse Parts His Mane.

Not good, but adequate.

Continue.

The White Crane Spreads Its Wings.

Adequate.

Pay no attention.

Don't think.

If you think about walking, you cannot walk. You can only think about walking.

The Heron Catches a Fish.

The forms flowed one into the next, blurring distinction.

The Black Fish Shows His Tail.

Vlod's pain subsided, and his grief returned to its rightful place.

The Warrior Draws His Sword.

Playing the Lute.

The Humpback Breaches.

Warding off an Attack.

The Cobra Strikes.

The Blue Heron—

"Stop, stop, stop!"

It was the sensei, Master Yokashima. In his arms, he was carrying a bundle of practice staves. How had he gotten so close without Vlod's hearing him?

Yokashima set the staves on the ground. "What form was that?"

Vlod slowly rose to his full height. "*The Blue Heron Hunts from a Piling.*"

"A local addition?"

"It's part of the Shaw Island Style," Vlod said. He wanted to explain, but he dared not lecture Master Yokashima.

"Continue!" The sensei's voice was noncommittal.

Vlod bowed and reentered the flow.

The Blue Heron Hunts from a Piling.

Holding a Single Whip.

The Cormorant Dries His Wings.

Patting the Horse's Back.

Taking—

"Stop! What form?"

"*Taking an Enemy's Head.*"

"A sword technique?"

"Or a palm edge," Vlod said. "The root techniques are identical."

"According to your way-masters."

"Yes, Sensei."

"I disagree. A hand is *not* a sword." After a moment, Yokashima said, "In any case, it is an ugly form."

"Death is never beautiful."

How easy it was to merge the form and the reality!

"Wrong! It is the form itself that is ugly. It interrupts the repose of the sages."

Taking a greater chance than he might have taken otherwise, Vlod said, "Perhaps, but it is effective."

Yokashima shrugged. "Warriors," he said, with good-natured contempt. "'Effective,' as though immediate results can compensate for such a loss. Tell me, Warrior, do you know the ninety-seven forms of the Shaw Island Style?"

"Yes," Vlod said.

"Do you have strength enough?"

Daring all, Vlod said, "Do you have youth enough?"

Yokashima arched an eyebrow, then he smiled. "The Style is eternal. You are not."

"Yes, Sensei."

"Very well, then," Yokashima said, and positioned himself next to Vlod. "Together! Opening stance! Begin! *The Wild Horse Parts His Mane...*"

Now that his muscles had limbered up, Vlod moved without interruption from posture to posture, from sequence to sequence.

Often the forms moved automatically, without his conscious thought or direction, reflexively shifting from one to the next, like the tides, like breathing, like the flow of prana through the chakras. At other times, Vlod had to concentrate on the sequence, to pay enough attention not to stray from the sequence but not so much attention as to drop out of the Style.

At the end of the Style, Yokashima looked carefully into Vlod's eyes, held his wrist, felt his brow. "You'll do," he said, "but eat lightly tonight."

"Yes, Sensei."

Yokashima was quiet for a long time. "It is a good style," he said, at last. "Useful. Not the style of a contemplative nor that of an academic, but it is that of a warrior. You did well to learn it."

"It's one of Wolfram's favorites."

"Naturally."

Yokashima picked up his bundle of practice staves and handed it to Vlod. "Break that in half!"

The bundle was fairly thick, and Vlod was certain it would be impossible for him to break it. The bundle was a dozen single staves bound together with twine. As individuals, they were thin and weak. Taken one at a time, they would be easy to snap. Taken as a whole, however, they would be next to impossible to break.

It was a familiar lesson, one of Wolfram's favorites. It was one that Vlod had learned so well he had forgotten it.

Vlod bowed very deeply and laid the bundle of staves at Master Yokashima's feet.

The impromptu lesson was over but the academic year was not. The cycle of class and study and examination continued, making its way through the fall, winter, and spring quarters.

Vlod ignored Mueller's snickering, Grady's jibes, and Royce's taunts. Instead, Vlod went to his favorite corner of the practice field whenever he could.

He did not seek the return of his father's books. Rather, he trained and waited.

SIXTEEN

In the weeks following that secret, nighttime funeral of a miscarried baby boy, various whispers made the rounds of the cathedral complex. Some genuinely worried, some frightened, some gloating, and some surprisingly hateful.

They travelled up and down the corridors and through the cathedral town, Maryhill. They moved like prowling wolves or slithering, hunting vipers.

If the avatar of the Goddess were to become unable to conceive, if she were to give birth to weaklings, or if she were to grow old, then the land itself would lose its fertility and its strength, and it, like the avatar herself, would turn barren.

No, the mother metropolitan cannot be a crone. By definition, she must be an active mother. She must give life to active, healthy, intelligent children.

In the end, the rumors and the whispers came to nothing.

Miscarriages were common, weren't they? It *was* a shame, but on the happier side, there was talk of a new building project, wasn't there? To grow some sort of fruit trees. Indoors. Indoors? How could that be possible? Trees are so big. Tomatoes, certainly, but whole fruit trees?

What perfect fun to see how it turned out! Aren't there such things as dwarf fruit trees? Yes, yes, that must be it. Dwarf fruit trees.

Thora's miscarriage was soon forgotten, together with the court's lingering worries about the crops, the fish runs, the prevalence of game, the regularity of the rain, and the depth of the mountain snowpack.

When Brenna turned sixteen, she spent her required year in the Virgins' Pavilion at the Cathedral Henge of Eileen the Immortal.

She'd tried to put it off and put it off, but the reminders had become insistence.

She soon discovered that she'd had good reason to have evaded the place. It was closer to livestock breeding or common prostitution than it was to a religious exercise.

At root, the Pavilion's routine both offended and bored her. How anyone could find meaning in such endless self-indulgence, in such narcissistic and affected sexual encounters, in such doe-eyed desperation to conceive, and in such endless contrived religious observances and specious rationalizations eluded her.

Not surprisingly, she was not much in demand.

For which she gave unending thanks.

Although she did her best, her honest best, to serve the Goddess, no matter her private attitude, to prove her fecundity, to become a *woman* of Clan Iredale, Brenna did not conceive.

The Rector of Virgins asked, "Have you given any thought to entering holy orders?"

Brenna's answer was automatic and to the point, "My path leads elsewhere."

"Where might that be?"

Not giving a direct answer, Brenna said, "Silk is no substitute for steel." This polite but direct answer wasn't a patch on what she had wanted to say.

Brenna returned to Fort George, to Olney Castle, to her own rooms, and to her own bed. She was home.

She renewed friendships, exchanged letters with Vlod, and went riding up in the hills and down on the beach. She went hunting to the south and to the east, and she went sailing on the river.

She went nowhere near the Iredale's manor henge, and she rebuffed each of Châtelaine Ameretat's attempts to talk with her, to console her, to comfort her.

Just as silk was no substitute for steel, a henge was no substitute for a battlefield.

When at last Brenna felt comfortable again in her own skin, when the compulsion to wash away the filth of the Virgin's Pavilion had faded, when her contempt for the Cathedral had waned, when her nightmares had begun to subside, she approached Wolfram and joined the clan's army.

SEVENTEEN

By the early fall of Vlod's sophomore year, in the twentieth year of her reign, it had become clear that Mother Metropolitan Thora had failed to conceive.

The year king, Guangli the Tranquil, had done everything humanly possible, but it was widely agreed that he lacked a certain quality that no one could adequately describe, much less name, and that it was the lack of this indefinable quality that was at fault.

The Feast of Mabon was nearly upon them, and the new fellow, the new year king, whoever he turned out to be, would doubtless be a man of unparalleled vigor.

Despite this optimism, new whispers, new rumors, and new fears ranged through the Cathedral. This time their paws hurried across the polished marble. Their nails made clicking, scratching sounds. They scraped furiously where they slipped, but they quickly regained traction. They left behind strands of hair that floated in the incense-scented air, adding their canine odor, the haunting scent of ravening wolves.

His fault or hers?

Did it matter?

No, she had missed.

Better a miss than a miscarriage.

Better a miss than another weakling.

That's true.

How many weaklings had there been?

Just the one. There'd been just that one, years ago.

Ah, yes. One, years ago.

A miss was indeed better than a weakling, but she *had* missed.

Aghast at the implications, Thora's allies protested that single years were often missed. For countless different reasons. Nursing often prevented conception. It was only to be expected. Thora had missed three of her expected years for that very reason, hadn't she? Her ninth, fifteenth, and seventeenth.

Despite their martial prowess, some year kings were simply more virile than others. Some were more, well, *interested* than others.

Her monthly flow hadn't stopped, had it?

No, it had not.

She had not dried up, had she?

No, she had not.

She was as *interested* as ever, wasn't she?

Yes, but she was older now.

But she could conceive, couldn't she? She was still capable, wasn't she?

She was.

Did any of that matter? She had missed.

Worldly, jaded smiles and shrewd rumors made the rounds.

The year king...

What about him?

Appetite was not virility.

Indeed, some seed never sprouts.

What about the women he had lain with? How many of them were pregnant?

Not many, they confessed.

Any miscarriages?

None.

Aha!

Yes, all was well with their beloved Thora. Give her time.

The rumors went silent, but Thora could not forget them. Nor could she deny the lines in the face staring back out at her from her mirror.

The Wheel was never still.

EIGHTEEN

At the Feast of Mabon that year, Duncan defeated Guangli, becoming the new year king. Guangli had been well liked, while Duncan, for all his masculine power, his raw presence, had taken a shocking amount of delight in his victories, especially in his slaughter of Guangli. *Slaughter*, for that is what it had been.

At the Academy, on the first day of the second week following Mabon, well after sunset, Vlod noticed his reflection in the bathroom mirror of room 305. It was a large mirror, rippled with age, but it gave a good reflection.

Vlod's face had lost the shadowed look that had taken root after the beating, after the theft of his father's books. Better, his eyes were clear and sharp, rested, and he saw in them a cold determination. His regret was gone, and the past spurred him forward.

The waiting and the training were over.

It was time for him to advance. It was time for him to become Wolfram when the Spitzenberg gap had opened.

Vlod pulled his cloak around his shoulders. It was a dark gray-green.

"Going out?" Aerian asked.

"For a while," Vlod said, and traded the light and warmth of room 305 for the dark and cold of the Academy's streets and alleys.

Royce would be the first. Work from the outside. Lap at the edges. Engage methodically.

Vlod must neither hurry nor scorn the tedious, necessary work of taking out the flankers.

True, it would warn, but true, it would also terrify, and those who are terrified make mistakes. They don't make as many as the arrogant, but runts can't be choosers.

Vlod found Royce not far from the public room attached to the main refectory.

Stepping into his path, Vlod said, "Hello, Royce."

"What do you want, runt?"

"It's time for you to return my books."

"Fuck you."

"Return them."

Royce answered with a palm strike, which Vlod avoided, and less than two seconds later, Vlod finished with *The Black Fish Slaps His Tail*.

In the morning, Vlod wrapped his right hand in a clean white cloth, to cover the damage to his knuckles, and went to class. Royce was absent.

Over lunch, Aerian asked, "Have you heard about Royce?"

"No. What?"

"Someone beat him up."

"What a shame," Vlod said, and refilled his coffee.

Royce returned to class at the end of the week. His cheekbone, where one of Vlod's blows had landed, carried a livid bruise that showed every sign of spreading down to his jaw.

When asked about it, he claimed to have stumbled into a closet door.

Vicious things, closet doors.

Late that night, when the sounds coming from the street told Vlod that the public room attached to the main refectory had begun to empty, he got up from his work and pulled on his dark gray-green cloak.

"Another midnight walk?" Aerian asked.

"It'll do me good."

"No doubt, but leave something for the infirmary to bandage."

Mueller was next.

The street glistened from an earlier rain squall that had moved on. The night torches threw orange smudges across the paving stones. It was the end of the week, time to unwind, time to relax, time to have a little fun.

Good idea...

Vlod approved of having a little fun.

Turnabout and so on.

Enough to underscore his determination.

With an inner sarcasm he did not believe in, he promised himself to act with as much humility as possible.

Mueller, whose appetites were never far from him, would have ridden down to the village for a whore, but he was equally unlikely to have stayed the entire night with her. He couldn't afford such luxuries.

Vlod found an alcove opposite the stables and waited.

A few minutes after the tower clock struck one, Mueller entered through the front gate. He rode into the stable, and bellowed for the groom to see to his horse.

How did the grooms put up with such cretins?

A good groom, never mind a good blacksmith, was worth ten student magi.

Vlod moved closer to the stable, wrapping himself in the shadows.

Perhaps their own self-respect made it possible for them to treat people like Mueller with the respect and obedience that they demanded but that they did not deserve, that they had not earned?

Mueller emerged and sauntered up the street. His stride was loose, and his arms swung in a natural rhythm. He was relaxed, not drunk, but completely at peace with himself and his world.

Vlod moved forward. He approached nearer and nearer to Mueller. He was so close that he could smell the tobacco smoke clinging to his clothes, smell the lingering traces of the whore's perfume, smell the spilled liquor.

Vlod tensed, flexing slightly, like a wolf about to spring.

A strong, hard-boned hand closed on Vlod's shoulder.

Vlod recognized the grip, that iron grip, and froze.

Master Yokashima.

Helplessly, Vlod watched as Mueller disappeared on up the street.

The sensei drew Vlod deeper into the shadows.

Shaking free, Vlod demanded, "What are you doing here?"

"Saving your useless, insignificant life."

In Yokashima's world lives had a tendency to be useless and insignificant.

"He was alone," Vlod said.

"You're not fighting a war," Yokashima said. "You nearly killed Royce."

"I did no such thing. He was back in class this morning, well, yesterday morning."

"You nearly killed him with your adolescent technique."

"I hit him where I intended."

"I'd expected better of you."

"I—"

"Don't evade!" Yokashima said. "Royce was a stooge, but Mueller was an eager participant. You would have killed him."

"I am in control."

"No, you are not. Go back to your room. Mueller is of no importance."

"But Grady is, and I have to go through Mueller to attack Grady. He has my father's books."

"Scraps of paper."

"The books were his."

"He was not his books," Master Yokashima said. He allowed a silence to form, to harden. He allowed it to draw out, allowed his lack of words to say everything else that needed to be said. When it had been, he gently added, "We have class tomorrow. Return to your room."

"Yes, Sensei."

As Vlod approached Palmer Hall, he saw Grady sitting on the front steps.

Vlod cycled his breath and continued toward the front door.

"You went after Mueller," Grady began.

Vlod decided that Grady had to have been watching from a nearby roof.

"Maybe I ought to have sold tickets," Vlod said.

Grady had then returned to Palmer Hall in time to intercept Vlod.

Grady said, "Too bad Yoki-Shoki stopped you."

"How's that?" Vlod asked.

"Royce and Mueller are fodder. I'm not."

"You're not?" Vlod asked. "That's news to me."

"You—"

"I want them back."

"Those 'scraps of paper'?" Grady laughed at him. "I'm not through with them yet. Who knows? Maybe I'll use them to wipe my ass. Maybe I already have!"

"Last chance," Vlod said.

"Duly noted."

"Good night, Not-Fodder," Vlod said, and went on up the stairs and into Palmer Hall.

In their room, Aerian was standing by the window.

"Quick!" Aerian said, and motioned for Vlod to join him at the window. "Down there, off to the left."

Yokashima and Grady were standing together on the far side of the quad. They were talking and laughing as though they were sharing a joke, as though they were the best of friends.

Vlod stood away from the window. "I don't believe it."

"Sorry," Aerian said. "Grady has been Yoki-Shoki's top student for the last two years."

***

In the morning, just before the clock struck the hour, Vlod filed onto the practice field with the rest of the second-year students. The weather was dry and cold. The air tumbled down the mountain, but the ground underfoot was slightly yielding and slightly damp. It was not a day for bare feet, but their feet were bare.

Grady stood at the front, next to Yokashima. The two of them watched the ranks form.

After the opening exercises, Yokashima said, "Grady, demonstrate *The Waxing Moon* kata."

"Yes, Sensei."

Grady's movements within the kata were quick and strong—too

quick and too strong. *The Waxing Moon* was a soft technique, not a hard one.

When Grady had completed his demonstration, he came to attention, relaxed and confident.

"Is *The Waxing Moon* appropriate to combat?" Yokashima asked him.

"As a foundation for combat, yes, Sensei!"

It was the standard answer for all katas.

What was Yokashima up to?

"Demonstrate!"

Grady smiled in anticipation. He made a show of surveying the class. Finally, he said, "Vlod? Will you assist?"

The muscles in the small of Vlod's back tightened.

Had Yokashima set one of them up?

Undoubtedly, but which?

"Of course," Vlod said, and trotted out from the ranks of students.

Grady and Vlod saluted Master Yokashima, then they saluted each other.

"Why don't you go home, runt?" Grady said.

"Because I have much to learn," Vlod replied.

Grady attacked in a series of feints and punches, each an elaborate attempt to intimidate. There was no humility in what he was doing.

Vlod refused to participate. He dodged and parried, but he refused to engage. If Grady chose to squander his strength in absurd theatrics, so be it. He would soon tire.

As Vlod refused either to advance or to retreat, either to fight or to concede. Grady's resulting bewilderment became strikingly apparent, and as it did, Vlod's nascent, barely acknowledged fear of the bully collapsed.

At the same time, his disgust with Grady's showy display flared. The man had as much substance as a thin coat of varnish.

Kick.

Parry...

Palm strike.

Deflect...

Flying kick.

Twist away…

Grady's attacks and Vlod's responses barely registered on Vlod's consciousness as distinct events. There was only the flow—the flow of the kata, the flow of battle.

Without any sort of warning, Grady backed away and broke his stance.

Was it a trap?

Maybe and maybe not. Either way, Vlod held his stance.

"Stop your dancing, runt," Grady said.

"I'm not your punching bag."

"I'm telling you to fight!"

"You're the one who's running his mouth."

"Resume!" Master Yokashima said. His tone was stern, uncompromising.

Grady resumed his stance.

Technically, his stance was correct, but the tone behind it was silly: He was posing.

Vlod neither attacked nor retreated. He stood, rooted, unmoving. He could sense no tension in his face, made no effort to focus his eyes on any particular thing. He drew his breath down into his body, and then exhaled from those same depths.

Time did not elongate, nor did it shorten. Instead, it remained as it had begun, flowing like a placid stream.

Vlod winked.

A simple wink.

Grady's face flashed from hostility to surprise to outrage.

Rather than a determined, serious attack, however, yet again he reverted to a series of kicks, punches, spins, and other moves that Vlod could only think of as an insulting, ego-driven display.

It was time for Grady to learn about the Iredales. Time and past.

Rather than block or divert the next of Grady's artful displays, which happened to be a kick aimed at Vlod's head, Vlod advanced inside the blow, turned, and elbowed Grady in the gut.

As Vlod had intended, the blow landed with enough force to drive the breath from Grady's lungs.

Vlod spun back in the opposite direction and with his other elbow hit Grady in the side of the head.

Grady staggered, doubled over, but was able to remain on his feet.

Moving easily, casually, Vlod turned again, clasped his hands together, forming a double fist.

He sensed, rather than heard, Yokashima change his stance. It was a subtle movement, the tightening of one set of muscles, the relaxation of another. Had Vlod been looking at his sensei, he was sure that there would have been nothing outward for him to see.

Control. Control was of the essence.

"Show me a defeated army," Wolfram invariably taught, "and I'll show you an army that lost control of itself."

Vlod relaxed the double fist and brought it down on the back of Grady's neck. This time, unlike he had with the two elbow strikes, Vlod pulled the punch, reducing it to a light tap.

Nevertheless, Grady's mouth flew open, his arms spread wide, as though he were trying to take flight. He flattened onto the ground.

He lay there, eyes wide, gasping for breath.

Vlod knelt and checked the pulse in Grady's neck. It was strong and regular. "You'll live," Vlod whispered.

He then stood and formally saluted Master Yokashima.

Yokashima nodded. "No better than acceptable."

"Thank you, Sensei," Vlod said.

Vlod saluted his sensei and returned to his place in the class.

Several moments later, the demonstration ended with a palpable draw, and Yokashima moved on to a succession of routine exercises. In his hands, however, they were anything but routine.

The tower clock chimed the three-quarter hour. The melody echoed across the Academy, and Yokashima dismissed the class.

He asked Vlod to remain.

"The double-fisted blow, you could have injured him," Yokashima said.

"I could have killed him, Sensei," Vlod said.

Vlod caught a memory of Grady, doubled over, helpless. Vlod remembered the joy of his victory over his tormentor, but he also remembered how that joy had shattered in the very moment of its achievement. He remembered the emptiness of it. He had relaxed his double fist and he had pulled the blow.

"Why didn't you?"

"Because you were right about the books and about me. Anyway, you wouldn't have permitted me to go as far as that."

"Could I have done so?"

Vlod allowed himself a slight, respectful smile. "Yes, I believe you could have."

"If you had killed him, I would have lost two good students, not just one. Despite his failings, Grady will one day make a fine magus."

Vlod found that hard to believe. "Tell me, Sensei, did you deliver me into his hands, or did you deliver him into mine?"

"Neither, you little fool," Yokashima said, his voice sparkling with delight. "I delivered both of you into *my* hands!"

That evening at dinner, fingers pointed, and rumors spread from table to table.

Vlod ate as naturally as he could, neither hurrying nor delaying, chatting with Aerian.

Later still, when Vlod returned to room 305 from the library, Aerian produced a package. "Here," he said, tossing it to Vlod. "Grady left it for you himself."

Vlod removed the heavy brown paper. It was his father's books, undamaged.

Aerian asked, "Any note?"

"No, just the books." Vlod's father's books. Not his father, but a link to him, to Vlod's memories of him, to, Vlod sensed, an explanation for his father's suicidal heresy.

Aerian said, "Grady's down in the public room. Why not buy him a drink and talk over old times?"

"Maybe another time," Vlod said. "He's in no mood to play the gracious loser, and I'm in no mood to put him through that."

"Even better!" Aerian said. "Welcome to the Academy, Runt. It's taken you a year to arrive, but now that you're here, welcome! I'm sure you'll do just fine."

Vlod noted the shift from *runt* as a slur to *Runt* as a nickname.

"Thanks." Vlod returned his father's books to their place on the shelf.

Reaching, finally, the absolute decision that would shape the balance of his life, he said, "I'm happy to be here."

Nineteen

Toward the end of Vlod's sophomore year at the Academy of Archmagus Basil the Anchorite and Wonderworker, Thora called Shabnan and Ulricka into her Terrace Room.

It was an afternoon in May. The breeze, what there was of it, came from the nearly treeless hillside above the Cathedral Henge of Eileen the Immortal. The air was hot and dry and smelled of parched grass. The weather was typical of a drought-plagued summer, not of a verdant spring.

Other aromas gamboled in the year's early heat: the pitch-heavy tang of the potted pines and junipers on the terrace outside the Terrace Room, the damp of the morning's watering, the sweet smell of roses and the ever-changing profusion of bedding plants ringing the terrace. Their colors offered a disciplined riot of orange, yellow, red, white, pink, and purple.

The breeze ghosting in through the open windows and doors caused the gauzy curtains to roll like dancers, slowly, sensuously turning, swaying, seducing.

Would Mabon never come? Would it never release her from her current dilemma and provide her with a new year king? The current specimen had been nicknamed Duncan the Pig, and with good reason.

He stank of sweat and filth and greasy food. His skin was slick with it, and his hair, which was black, shone with yet more grease. His own. It oozed from his scalp...and every other part of him.

Tonight she would overcome her loathing. She would take him into her bed, take him into her, and then, possibly, the rumors would dissipate. For a time.

Once they began they never stopped.

Her predecessor, Alrys, had told her about those rumors, and now, thanks to the turning of the Wheel, Thora knew about them for herself, understood them in a way that no amount of instruction could impart.

May...

Year kings were an eager lot, but as the summer took hold and the fall approached, as the days began noticeably to shorten, they became frantic.

Four months, and then, with any luck, Duncan the Pig would be gone and a new man would reign as the mortal and immortal God. More, much more, the new man would *be* the God, the year king, the Divine Consort, His avatar.

Four months.

Thora could almost feel sorry for Duncan the Pig.

Almost.

He was such a wretched, repulsive thing.

She was amazed that he didn't snort and eat from a trough.

It was an interesting notion, but other matters demanded her attention. She would have to leave Duncan and his trough for another time.

Her guests had arrived and she must attend to them.

The business at hand could no longer wait.

The Wheel was near, very near to turning yet again.

Thora, Shabnan, and Ulricka strolled, so very casually, out onto the room's north-facing terrace, the one crowded with shade-loving plants, and sat in the redundant shelter of an awning.

They ate thin slices of bread and blackberry jam, and they drank cold, amber-colored beer. The bread and the jam had come from the pantry. The beer had come straight from the chilling racks in the icehouse. The icehouse was a cave cut deep into the hillside and lined with basalt blocks—a storehouse for the winter's ice. Thora thought that such a facility, an icehouse, was an expensive, petty luxury, but she enjoyed the cold beer.

Petty, too, would be the luxury of greenhouse-grown oranges or a life extended beyond its purpose, extended beyond the tipping point between devotion and sacrilege, between worship and blasphemy, where each heartbeat was an abomination.

From where the three of them sat, they could see the cobblestone road that led up to the icehouse. Slabs of Newcastle Island sandstone framed the entrance, and a large iron-bound wooden gate closed out the heat and sealed in the cold.

Farther on up that hillside, above the icehouse, a small, controlled herd of buffalo were grazing. They were protected, fed when appropriate, culled when their numbers grew too large. They were as much pets as they were anything else.

Now and then they wandered away, but never far. They were not wild. They might not be the brightest things on Earth, but they weren't stupid.

To Ulricka, Thora said, "Tell me, Ricki, are you happy here?"

"You mean to do it, then?" Shabnan asked.

"Do what?" Ulricka asked, the color suddenly draining from her face.

The color had drained from Thora's face when Alrys, Thora's predecessor, had put that same question to her. It was the innocent-sounding opening of a death sentence.

"If she'll have it, yes," Thora said. "The whole truth, Ricki. The *whole* truth. Are you *happy* here?"

Thora sipped her beer, peering over the rim of her glass. It was a naked ploy. She was giving Ulricka time to frame her answer, and she was giving herself time to steel herself to hear it. She must not lose this one. She must set the hook and play her in. It was for her own good, and the Province deserved no less. The child had backbone.

"The whole truth?" Ulricka said. "I wonder what that is." She sipped her beer, brows furrowed. She was obviously putting off answering the question. Finally, she said, "Yes, I'm happy here. I'm a Child of the Cathedral. I could have left, but I've stayed. I've never wanted to be anywhere else. Oh, I don't like—"

Thora made a dismissive gesture. "Never mind your list," she said. "We all have them, and they're all the same, give or take." Again she sipped her beer. It was pleasant, but a trifle sweet. "I can recite it for you by heart. You hate the politics, but you love the Cathedral Henge."

"Well, I do," Ulricka said, a shade too defensively.

She would have to learn to curb that self-indulgence, that reflexive flight to self-defense.

Thora had to smile. How like that long-ago Thora she sounded, that child who dwelt in the adult Thora's memory, squirming under Alrys' unflinching, iron-fisted gaze.

How unspeakably cruel that woman had been!

Cruel?

No.

Determined.

Aware.

Unflinching.

"What's so funny about my loving the Henge?" Ulricka demanded.

"Nothing," Shabnan said. "Not a thing."

Thora asked, "The question is, how much do you love it? Do you love it enough to spend the rest of your life devoted to it?"

Ulricka's answer was long—too long?—in coming, and when it did, it was an equivocation. "Yes, I suppose so. What makes you think I wouldn't?"

"Would you do it gladly or out of a sense of duty?"

This time Ulricka fired her answer back too quickly. "Gladly!"

She was veering from one extreme to the other. Could anything she said be trusted? Thora decided to press the issue. "Do you love it enough to give up having a husband and children of your own, your own to love, your own to raise, your own to watch grow up? Are you willing to give them up, that husband and those children, for the sake of the Province? For the sake of the Goddess and the God?"

Ulricka's face looked as though she were facing a headsman. "What's going on?" Ulricka asked.

"Vladika, you ought to have prepared the poor girl," Shabnan said.

"Nonsense," Thora said. "It's better this way. Catch her off guard and pry the truth out of her. Deliver it by Cesarean section if need be."

"The truth about what?" Ulricka asked, her voice rising in pitch and volume.

More than she'd meant it to?

"The Cathedral," Thora said. "The Goddess. The God. Would you give up everything for them?"

"I've already told you I would!" Ulricka said. She was close to shouting now. "Yes, yes, yes, I'd sacrifice everything for them. Gladly. What else do you want me to say?"

"It's not a matter of what I *want* you to say," Thora said. "It's a matter of what's in your heart."

"What's going on?"

"Would you die for them?"

"I'm not answering that. First you tell me what's going on. Why all the questions? Am I under suspicion?"

A touch of genuine hysteria had crept into Ulricka's voice, and Thora wondered whether or not she'd made the right choice.

"Calm down, Ricki," Thora said. "Nothing's wrong. I'm going to make you a châtelaine with labrys and crosier. We'll have to ordain you to the priesthood first, but we can accomplish that in an afternoon."

Shabnan bobbed her head in Ulricka's direction, a mocking, teasing gesture. "Welcome to the Holy Synod, your grace. Many years!"

What little color remained in Ulricka's face left it. "I don't—"

"The Synod will do as I tell them, which means they'll approve. The Congregation of Priestesses and Priests will assent to their decision." Thora smiled triumphantly. "We'll have you consecrated before the month is out."

"Ah, just in time for the month of June," Shabnan said. "June is such a lovely month for travelling. Warm enough not to be cold, but cool enough not to be hot. Delightful month, June."

"You're sending me away?" Ulricka wailed.

"No, as a matter of fact, I'm not."

"But, Vladika, if you're not, then where is her châtellenie to be?" Shabnan asked. "You have to send her somewhere, don't you? Down-river I expect, or perhaps up." In feigned surprise, as though she'd just that moment uncovered a profound secret, she said, "You wouldn't dare send her upriver to Narmer's lands, would you? That would be too cruel for words."

"You've had your fun," Thora said.

"Yes, Vladika," Shabnan said, not the least bit humbled.

Turning back to Ulricka, Thora said, "I can't have you as a titular châtelaine. You must have a see, something to *do*. Otherwise, there's no point in my bestowing a crosier. Labrys *and* crosier, that's you."

"You're sending me away," Ulricka said again, her voice stricken.

Thora's gut was spinning. She had to keep the tone as light as possible, a touch of teasing, a touch of friendly sarcasm, albeit now and then thoroughly caustic. Shabnan wasn't helping, though. The Crone, bless her, did so delight in overplaying her role.

"No, I'm not sending you away," Thora said. "You're to be the châtelaine of the Châtellenie of Maupin and Warm Springs."

"Oh, how splendid!" Shabnan said happily. "You're making her an apostle to the Brethren. Wonderful!" Shabnan tilted her glass in Ulricka's direction. "Cheers, my dear! It's the mission field for you."

"I won't go!" Ulricka shouted.

"Oh, yes, my darling girl, you will," Thora said, without a hint of irony in her voice, for Ulricka was her darling girl and she was destined to work among the Brethren, for now. "Never fear. You'll be able to oversee your territories from right here at the Cathedral."

"For the most part," Shabnan said. "You'll have a splendid opportunity to travel to new and interesting places." Those new and interesting places were out on the fringes of the Province, out among the snake cultists and tree worshipers. Why was it always snakes and trees? Shabnan scoffed at her own question. Why was it always dying and reviving Gods? Why was blood the key to every sacred act?

"I see," Ulricka said. Her voice was stiff and cold.

"No, you don't," Thora said, "but one day you will." She sipped her beer. It was still cool, but the pleasure had gone out of it. She was condemning this girl, this child. The reality that she had no other choice, given the options available, did nothing to mollify her guilt.

An attendant appeared in the doorway. She was sixteen or a little older, slight, thin-boned, brown hair, not homely but not pretty, either. She was about the age that Ulricka had been when Thora had singled her out, had spotted the depth of intellect lurking behind those splendid, mesmerizing eyes, and had shifted her from favorite to protégé. But this girl, also a Child of the Cathedral, a henge brat, was as dull as yesterday's oatmeal. She wasn't stupid, but she had no spark. She served and asked no questions, made no plans. She did as she was told, no more and no less.

"Your Beatitude, it's three o'clock," the attendant said. Her voice was correct but lifeless.

And with that, the day's work returned to its normal course.

In the corridor outside the Terrace Room, Shabnan said, "Walk with me, Ricki. You have questions, and I have answers."

TWENTY

At Shabnan's direction, she and Ulricka left the Saraswati Palace through a side entrance and turned downhill.

They made their way through the precincts of the Cathedral Henge, which was on the north side of the Columbia River.

The precincts were distinct from the cathedral town, Maryhill. They were a walled district of their own.

For reasons that Shabnan didn't care to go into, Maryhill was rapidly growing into an independent city. The precincts were growing, too, but they were accomplishing this by adding stories and linking the upper floors of the buildings with bridges.

The downward slope faced to the south, toward the river, and they had the afternoon sun on their faces.

Shabnan couldn't speak for Ulricka, but as far as she was concerned, the warm sun was a welcome change after a spring that had so far brought profligate amounts of rain. It would be weeks before the ground dried.

The streets between the buildings were warm, but not oppressive, laden with the powerful stench of animal dung and horse urine.

The odor threatened to blister Shabnan's nose and sinuses. Breathing through her mouth didn't do any good because when she did, not only could she still smell that foul stench, but she could also taste it.

Black flies buzzed around the piles of excrement, landing, crawling, feeding, laying their eggs; while dragonflies darted back and forth.

In the shadowed spaces, the mosquitos were already out, whining around Shabnan's ears, questing about her neck and arms, landing, intent on biting, sucking, feeding. Time and again, she brushed them away or swatted them, gladly, into the next world.

The two women walked by clusters of utilitarian buildings: offices, counting houses, warehouses, workshops, stables, and guards' barracks.

For the time being, most of them were being left as they were, but several were having one or more floors added.

The women passed tall, ornate buildings: rectories, monasteries, convents, and officers' apartment blocks. And they went by less ornate, shorter buildings: dormitories, dining halls, and immediate-access commissaries.

The fruit stands hummed with the ear-stabbing whine of yellow jackets, and the complex's one butcher shop reeked of blood, filthy sawdust, entrails, and raw meat. Here the flies were at their frantic, insistent worst.

Finally, the two women exited the cathedral precincts, passing out through the Southern Gate and entering Maryhill.

Here the streets widened, the buildings were taller, and the heat lessened.

Shabnan stopped at a flower stall and bought two small bouquets. Daffodils and purple irises predominated.

Shabnan handed one to Ulricka. "Take these."

"Why are you giving me a bouquet?" Ulricka said.

"So you can leave them for someone else."

Shabnan led Ulricka to the east, through the town.

Eventually they reentered the cathedral precincts via Vancouver's Gate.

They angled up the side hill, following the Pilgrims' Road. It was a wide track, slate-paved, and curbed with marble. Geometric red-brick designs traced along its center.

To their right, the hill sloped away in an expanse of lawn and trees—

firs, maples, and willows—that ended at a stone wall. Above them, to their left, beyond a waist-high granite retaining wall and beyond another expanse of lawn, but without trees, soared the Cathedral Henge of Eileen the Immortal.

The Henge proper consisted of concentric rings of towering stone monoliths that were capped and connected by equally massive lintels. At the moment, sky-blue banners emblazoned with multicolored devices, in the manner of ideographs, mystically committed prayers and intercessions to the care and charge of the Four Winds, who would deliver them to the Gods and the Generations.

In a few days, at the Dark Moon, the banners would change to white, in anticipation of the coming Full Moon, and the Four Winds could capture and carry aloft another set of prayers and entreaties.

"Vancouver's Gate," Shabnan said. "For whom is it named?"

"Vancouver," Ulricka said.

"Oh, how very perceptive of you. Who was he?"

Silence.

"This path is the Pilgrims' Road," Shabnan said. "Who named it?"

Silence, then, "I can't remember."

The truth struck Shabnan like a bolt of summer lightning. "You never knew," Shabnan said, as brutally as she could.

These lessons were too important to be trivialized, and this child— never mind her chronological age—was too important to be allowed to ignore them.

It was time for her to grow up. As quickly as she could. If she could. If she was willing to make the effort. If she was willing to shoulder the risks and take on the inexhaustible *work*.

That was a cautionary maze.

Why would she be willing? Why *should* she? Because Thora had asked her to? Because of what she had so obviously *not* been taught?

The whole thing was too frustrating for words!

For the love of Heaven! Ulricka was a henge brat. The Cathedral's primary and secondary schools had given her a basic education, hadn't hey? She'd graduated from the Cathedral's seminary. For the love of Heaven, she'd been in and around the theology and history of the faith and of the Cathedral her entire life.

But she had retained none of it!

Nothing of any lasting importance!

Her faith, her own faith, was unknown to her.

Well, that stopped right now!

Shabnan stopped and pointed up at the Cathedral Henge. "That is the Cathedral Henge of Eileen the Immortal."

"I know what—"

"Then *who* was she? Why is she called 'the Immortal'? What else is named for her?"

With a disappointing hint of smugness, Ulricka said, "She was the Goddess' first authentic prophet following the Second Creation. The Pool of Eileen is also named for her."

"Which is where?"

"Downstream. On the Manor Island."

Shabnan shook her head. "Better, but not nearly good enough. Why is she called 'the Immortal'?"

"I—"

"There's no excuse for your abysmal ignorance. You ought to have been taught, and you may have been, but you never *learned*. You ought to have read it for yourself, but you never did."

Shabnan turned her back on the goggling child and strode on. Without looking back, she shouted, "Keep up! The Wheel is turning. Take care lest the Goddess crush you beneath its tire."

Ulricka hurled the bouquet of flowers onto the path. "I won't be bullied. Not by you. Not by anyone!" She turned and started back down the path.

Shabnan caught up to her, spun her around, and slapped her.

The whole of it transpired in one fluid motion, a single motion of many parts, like a dance step.

The blow landed squarely and solidly and produced a remarkably loud *Pop!*

The blow, for that was what it was, left behind an outline of Shabnan's hand on the girl's face.

Given the severity of that slap, the self-absorbed little ninny *might* remember the whole of the afternoon: what had happened, what had been said, and what was about to happen.

Ulricka, mouth open, eyes brimming, face red, was trembling in terror.

But she wasn't whimpering, and she wasn't throwing a fit.

Thora would have been pleased to see it.

"You, child, have two choices," Shabnan said. She held up her index finger. "First, you can pick up those flowers and continue our walk." She added her next finger. "Or, second, you can leave the flowers where they are and turn back. You can return to your apartment and hang yourself." She dropped her hand. "You have no other options."

"Why would I kill myself?"

"Because you'd be doing yourself a favor."

"You can't—"

"If you turn back at this point, you're finished. It might take you a lifetime to realize it, but eventually you'll understand that you should have continued on." Shabnan paused. "Is that too complicated for you, *child*?"

"Not in the least."

"Good. When you do realize it, as you surely will, on that day, you'll wish, you'll pray, with every desiccated fiber of your shriveled being, that you'd never lived. You'll pray for death. You'll long for it. You'll yearn for it. You'll beg for it as you've never begged for anything in your long, empty, self-centered, meaningless, self-indulgent, evil, fear-driven life."

"What makes you think I will?" Ulricka shot back, a new note of defiance in her voice, in her stance.

Shabnan leaned in very close to the child, close enough to smell the traces of beer on Ulricka's breath, the remnants of the perfume she'd put on that morning, the bitterness of the sweat that had formed on her body during the warm afternoon.

Hitting each of her words, timing them deliberately, Shabnan said, "Because when I was called, I turned back!"

"I'm not *you*."

"What possible difference does that make?"

They stood silently for a time. The wind, what there was of it, hissed in the fir needles and rattled in the maple leaves. The willow branches stirred.

Shabnan's mouth was dry and tasted of dust. It tasted of the grave, and she feared that she might have overplayed her hand.

Thora had the right of that. Shabnan loved a scene, and she was too prone to give herself over to the flow and rhythm of her own words.

Yes, it was true. She was too easily enthralled by the sound of her own declamations. On the other hand, was that such a bad trait for a Crone of the Cathedral to have?

Shabnan thought not.

The child stood there, her feet rooted, staring, mystified. Stupid beyond belief.

High above them, an eagle cried, hauntingly, issuing a challenge of its own. It left one branch and swooped toward another. Landing, it gripped the branch with its talons, gripped and held, settling effortlessly on its new perch.

Ulricka stooped and picked up the flowers.

Together, the two women walked on.

The path curved up the hillside.

They came to a turnoff. The main path continued on up to the plaza skirting the Henge. It was a steeper rise, majestic, commanding. It had been intended to awe and to inspire. The branching path angled gradually on across the side hill toward the Sacred Grove.

Shabnan followed the turning, toward the Sacred Grove.

Here trees lined both sides of the path and the paving changed from slate to clinker brick. The bricks were dark red in the afternoon light.

"Who was Samuel Hill?" Shabnan asked.

"The builder of the innermost ring," Ulricka said.

"Of the original innermost ring," Shabnan said.

"The *original*? I thought—"

"There have been extensive modifications," Shabnan said. "What else? What else did he build?"

"I don't know."

"You'll learn. There's a reason why the Cathedral is located here. A root cause for why it grew here, organically, spontaneously, rather than by fiat. Without intending it—and probably to his horror were he here to learn of it—he is that root cause."

"How? What are your talking about?"

"Never mind," Shabnan said. "I've plagued you sufficiently for one day. But take heart. There's more to come."

They entered the Sacred Grove itself, and, as though guided by a spectral attendant, they found the grave of Thora's miscarried son. A yellow rosebush marked it.

Ulricka asked, "Why did you bring me here?"

"So you'll remember," Shabnan said.

"I'll never forget that night."

"The Wheel is never still and memory is a fickle bitch."

The fragrance of the roses, some in bud and some in bloom and some blown, filled the air. Their spent petals littered the ground, like fallen leaves.

Shabnan and Ulricka placed their flowers at the base of the bush.

"Did Thora plant the rose?" Ulricka asked.

"No, I did that," Shabnan said, "But she added his name to the *Dirge* herself. Micah. She wrote it in with her own hand."

Ulricka didn't answer, but stood staring at the rosebush, at the grave. Ulricka had never heard of such a thing, adding a name to the *Dirge Common to the Cathedral Henge of Eileen the Immortal* by fiat. It couldn't be canonical, and yet Thora had done it, and no one had objected. No one had called for an inquiry. No one.

"It was a touching scene," Shabnan said. "The Mistress of Sojourners protested, but what else could she do. It was her duty to protest. The child had miscarried. Therefore, he had never been born; therefore, he had never been ontologically named; therefore, there was no name to enter into the *Dirge*."

Ulricka looked bewildered, as though her attempt to follow that simple train of logical steps had caused her to have a migraine.

If she only knew what awaited her!

Shabnan continued, "Vladika overruled her. She made threats—quite graphic ones—and promises, too, and so, in the end, the Mistress stood aside and Thora did the deed herself." Shabnan left a pause, then added, "The dirge singers chanted his name as only they can when they put their minds to it."

"I've heard them when they chant like that," Ulricka said, as though wrapped in a memory.

Shabnan chose not to follow up on that revelation.

"I have something else to show you," Shabnan said. "You've seen it before—countless times—but this time I want you to see it with open eyes. I want you to *see* it. Do you understand?"

"I think so."

"I doubt that," Shabnan said, not unkindly. "What I'm asking you to do is to see your mirror image for the *first* time."

They retraced their steps, walking back along the brick-paved walkway.

When they came to the junction, rather than going down into the town, they turned uphill toward the Henge Mount.

They came to another junction. One branch led up, via a board ramp, onto the plaza on the Henge Mount, while the other branch circled on around its base. They followed the second branch, the more gradual path. It tracked clockwise, circling around the base of the mount.

To their left the ground slanted away in a sweep of green lawn. It sloped all the way down to the Pilgrim Road, the road they had come up.

To their right rose the Wall of the Year Kings.

Shabnan invariably found the wall disquieting or worse. Often enough she found it an outright challenge to the remaining dregs of her sense of piety.

Faith was entirely too fragile, too easily undermined.

Without doubt, however, without spiritual caution, without religious conservatism, fanaticism was sure to rear its ugly head. Take Narmer, that Egyptophile chieftain whose land lay farther upriver. He was a perfect example. He was a man with few doubts. The result? He was also a fanatic of the first water, a fraud who'd packed his court with fawning sycophants, bootlickers, and cowards. There wasn't a backbone in the whole lot.

Whatever else might be said of the year kings, they had courage. They had backbone, as did Ulricka, when she chose to straighten it.

Shabnan told herself that in bald architectural terms, the Wall of the Year Kings was an ordinary retaining wall. It stood several meters high and was faced with, first, multicolored sandstone blocks and, second, with black, white, and pink granite slabs. The slabs were highly polished and esthetically pleasing, given what they truly were.

As for its root purpose, the wall retained the fill that had been used, centuries ago, to expand the Henge Mount, to create a large table of land onto which the Cathedral and its immediate grounds could be extended.

And, indeed, as intended, in the center of the mount stood the Henge. The structure was living theology in stone. It was the place where the eternal and the temporal crossed over, where they intermingled, touched, and, like lovers, became one.

The Wall of the Year Kings, however, was also a mausoleum. Within it, the crypts marked by brass plaques, lay each of the year kings, every last one. They stretched from Vancouver the Progenitor to Guangli the Tranquil, last year's year king. In time, in a few months or a year or two at most, the current year king, Duncan the Pig, would join them.

Sooner would be better than later.

So and blessed let it be!

She scanned the plaques, and a new thought occurred to her. It couldn't be a *new* thought, but it was new to her. Well, *new* to her in its current intensity.

The thought was an observation: In a very literal way, it was the year kings who held the Cathedral Henge of Eileen the Immortal in place, who held it aloft, up there on its hilltop, for all to see.

Shabnan filed the power of that thought away. She dared not call it an insight, much less a conviction, not yet. It was the mothers metropolitan who stood at the center of the Cathedral's work, at the center of the religion, but it was the year kings who...who what?

Here she came up short. She could recite their various functions, practical and theological. But beyond that recitation she found, to her horror, that she had nothing to add.

Veering away from that swamp, she tried to see the wall as a whole.

She failed.

Instead, she could see only the individual plaques.

The Cathedral Henge, the Henge Mount, the Wall of the Year Kings —it was all so very deeply moving, or was meant to be, but it was also all so very deeply frightening, whether it was meant to be or not.

By its very design, the Cathedral Henge had been intended to instill religious awe. Had it also been intended to engender a sense of personal terror, a sense that at any moment the Goddess was capable of reaching out, through the Cathedral Henge, through the veil of Her creation, Her Second Creation, and crushing the life out of anyone and everyone who displeased Her? Did their intentions matter to Her? How did their frailties weigh in the balance? She could not overlook them, but neither could She ignore them, not and maintain any sort of moral order.

Had the prompting of that sense of moral hazard, that feeling of terror, been, not an *additional* purpose, but the *true* purpose of the Cathedral Henge? Was *awe* simply another word for *terror*, for fear in the face of divine wrath?

Shabnan didn't believe, couldn't believe for one second, that the Goddess would ever behave in such a manner, would ever inspire such a motive, such a gross travesty of theology and piety and mercy, such a betrayal of Her revelation of Herself.

But the Goddess *had* sent the Great Winter. She *had* wiped out most of what had been alive on the Earth. She had thus cleared the way for the Second Creation. Unquestionably, the Second Creation had been and was Her reassertion of Her dominion over what was, indisputably, Her creation.

And so Shabnan told herself that it was entirely appropriate, entirely reasonable, for her to feel not merely religious awe but also pure terror.

She found it an unhappy but reassuring conclusion.

From where the two women were walking, only the tops of the Henge's lintels were visible.

The lowering sun shone on the brass plaques attached to the Wall of the Year Kings, the memorials of those interred behind them.

The women came to a plaque framed with ornate bas-relief columns and arches. The plaque was not brass, but gold.

VANCOUVER
1 TO 29
Memory Eternal

Shabnan asked, "Do you know who Vancouver was?"

"The first year king," Ulricka said.

"He was the first year king *that we know of*. There may have been others, but they've gone unrecognized. Can you tell me why he reigned for twenty-nine years?"

"He was skilled in combat?"

"You're guessing," Shabnan said. She sighed. "We ought to leave off now. We can pick this up later."

"Thank you," Ulricka said.

As an afterthought, Shabnan asked, "You're not a hunter, are you?"

"No, I don't hunt."

"Thora's invited you, hasn't she?"

"Yes, but I'm a terrible shot."

"Learn," Shabnan said. "I'll talk to her. When she asks again, accept."

"I don't—"

"I think you'd find it grounding."

Her expression changing, Ulricka said, "I'll be happy to go, and in the meantime, I'll begin practicing."

The child was learning. "Wise choice."

TWENTY-ONE

One of the attendants brought a coffee service into Thora's sitting room, but it was His Honor, the Venerable Jinhai, Archdeacon, Protopriest, and Archthurifer of the Cathedral Henge of Eileen the Immortal who poured.

The attendant was one of the fluttering variety, the service was one of the ornate silver variety, and Thora's sitting room was one of the light-and-airy variety. As much as Jinhai loved Thora, he despised the room.

It was supposed to be a comfortable place in which to while away anything from a quarter of an hour to an entire afternoon, a place to entertain without the constrictions imposed by places such as the palace's drawing room, dining room, or ballroom.

The sitting room's crisp lines, expansive windows, gleaming floors and walls, brass door handles, and its angled, functional furniture, taken as a whole, in a single mental sweep, reminded Jinhai of the inner workings of a metal machine, a sanitized, inhuman clockwork.

Only Thora's presence rendered the chamber even remotely bearable.

The room was, Jinhai mused, only slightly better than one of those fluttering attendants. They were like locusts masquerading as butterflies.

Thora drank her coffee black, while Jinhai preferred his with both cream and sugar.

In terms of its aroma and taste, the coffee was a match for the room, only the coffee was pleasantly hot and organic. One could imagine the coffee as having had an origin in or of the earth. The same could not be said for the Mother Metropolitan's sitting room.

This was an illusion. The wood had come from trees. The stone had come from quarries. The metal had come from mines. The preparation, construction, and finishing work had been done with both human and animal labor. Nothing in or about the room was in fact artificial.

Setting down her cup of coffee, Thora said, "I'd like your opinion."

"Of what?"

"At this stage, it's very preliminary, and it might not work out, but..." Her voice trailed away, like the voice of an embarrassed adolescent.

"Go on," Jinhai said.

"I want to nominate Ulricka to become a châtelaine."

Jinhai felt the muscles around his eyes tighten. He cursed himself for not having anticipated this. Roisin's untimely death had created a vacancy in the Sobor, and now Thora was filling it.

Doing his best to be agreeable without playing the sycophant, he said, "Ulricka is quite well thought of."

Thora nodded. "Are you damning her with faint praise, old friend?"

They were closer than friends, and yet, they could be no better than friends. Lifelong companions? Man and wife? Never. The Gods and the Generations had chosen differently for them.

Making a dismissive gesture, Jinhai said, "Well, she *is* well thought of."

Thora nearly frowned. "But not by you."

Jinhai smiled as disarmingly as he knew how. "Regrettably, no, not by me."

"You aren't jealous of her, are you?"

Jinhai chose to evade that abattoir of sanity. "Which châtellenie?" he asked.

"Maupin and Warm Springs. Your thoughts?"

Jinhai sighed. Perhaps sanity had been fated to fly out the window from the start. "She wouldn't have been my first choice."

"I agree, but the field is painfully narrow."

"Widen it."

"Where would you have me look?"

"In the usual places."

"That's where I found her."

Jinhai wanted to make a cutting remark about Thora's bed being the place where she'd found Ulricka, but such a comment would have been worse than pointless, and it would have betrayed the depth of his jealousy.

He sipped his coffee. "The usual places outside of the Cathedral, then: the manor henges, the monasteries, and the shrines. Among the lesser clergy."

"The new châtelaine will have to be intimate with the Cathedral's comings and goings."

"For Maupin and Warm Springs?" Jinhai asked. The words were scarcely out of his mouth when the full extent of what he'd been told, of what Thora had asked him, struck home. How suddenly the time had passed! How quickly it would draw to a close! But Ulricka? Thora couldn't be that naïve. "Do you mean for her to succeed you?"

"Nothing's settled."

Which meant that everything was settled. She wasn't searching for advice, but for reassurance. "Ulricka's too arrogant," Jinhai said.

"You're misreading her."

"Goddess grant," Jinhai said.

"But?"

Jinhai had no reason to evade, no reason to back away at this point. "She's arrogant because she's afraid." The last scrap of his reserve shattered. "Those fears will lead her to maneuver when she ought to stand her ground, to follow when she ought to lead, and to acquiesce when she ought to dominate."

"And?"

"Despite her best intentions, she'll throw the Province into chaos."

"Very prettily said."

She refilled their coffees.

"I hope I'm wrong," Jinhai said.

"Yes, old friend, let's hope you are, because it's going to be Ulricka."

"Why? Why must it be Ulricka?"

"Because there's no one else, either inside or outside of the Sobor. Don't you think I've looked?"

"I can't imagine that you haven't."

"I'll grant you she has her problems," Thora said. "We all do. Nevertheless, beneath her bluster, she has genuine courage."

"I'll take your word for it."

"I wish she didn't."

"Why's that?"

"Because...Well, never mind why," Thora said. She bolted down the last of her coffee. "Will you come to me tonight?"

"Of course," Jinhai said. "I was hoping you'd ask."

Twenty-Two

At the end of their walk, Ulricka returned to the palace, but Shabnan returned to the Grove.

Had the walk helped?

Shabnan couldn't say, not for sure, but by all appearances, the scope and import of Ulricka's situation had begun to dawn on the poor girl.

And a good thing, too, if Shabnan were any judge, and she fancied that she was.

The Crone walked between the massive, ancient oaks until she came to the Grove's absolute center, its living heart.

Here in an area of open ground were the graves of the mothers metropolitan. Chiseled stone markers, low to the ground, marked them.

Shabnan gazed down at the marker on Alrys' grave, then at the space next in line.

This place, this untouched plot, ought to have been Shabnan's. Here, right here, but for one life-searing moment of cowardice, was where she ought to have been laid to rest. Interred years ago. But not such a great many of them. Ten perhaps.

She had been Alrys' first choice, not Thora, but Shabnan had refused the nomination. She had claimed that she was too old, but the truth was that she had been too afraid of dying.

But whether Shabnan was the Mother Metropolitan or not, as with Alrys, as with Thora, every year was bringing her own death inescapably nearer.

So be it.

She would face it when it came.

She was not yet ancient, not yet stooped, blind, sagging, senile, or wrinkled beyond recognition. She was not yet beyond another's desire.

No, not yet. Soon, but not today.

Had they begun to carve Thora's tombstone? Surely Thora had made her selection of the stone to be used. Shabnan had seen the samples herself, had helped with the selection, but had the stone carvers put their chisels to it?

By this time, their tools had to be sharp, but then, they always were. They knew no respite.

Walking back toward the Saraswati Palace, Shabnan decided that she ought to renew her own interest in hunting, in archery at the very least. She could do with a bit of grounding.

And, too, with the three of them in the field, nothing on four legs would be safe. Except for those wretched buffalo, but bringing down one of those *ruminants* wouldn't be worth the price of the arrows.

Twenty-Three

The weather in the fall of Vlod's junior year at the Academy of Archmagus Basil the Anchorite and Wonderworker was mild, with warm days and little rain. The clear skies meant colder nights, but those were a small price for dry clothes and dry boots.

In addition to the usual revelries, the Feast of Mabon had seen Duncan the Pig's defeat by Izanagi, a champion from upriver, one of Narmer's protégés.

It was rumored that before the final match one or another of Thora's inner circle had dosed Duncan with so much valerian that he could barely lift his sword. The valerian, however, had not prevented him from bellowing like a stuck pig and bleeding out in record time.

Had they hedged their bets by coating Izanagi's blade with poison? It would have made sense if they had.

Down on the lower stretches of the Columbia River the gentle weather was a special boon. Freighters, barges, and the fishing fleets jumped at the chance to keep their pace up.

The late fall crops were abundant, and logging and lumber milling raced ahead.

At the mouth of the river, the number of bar crossings, both inbound and outbound, surpassed their late-summer levels. Soon enough the winter would close in, but in the meantime there was freight to load, freight to haul, and freight to deliver.

Yokashima took advantage of the unusual weather to drill his students in the open air. He scheduled extra sessions and demonstrations in the late afternoons and early evenings.

It was often after dark before he released his weary students.

In fairness, however, many of these sessions were filled with the sensei's stories of his homeland and of his adventures, how he had ended up, for the time being, at the Academy.

The good luck couldn't last, and it didn't.

———

One bright afternoon, Ziellottes arrived with word that Morven, Edmund's son and heir, had been killed in a cattle raid.

Ziellottes pulled Vlod out of his class on augury and divination to deliver the news.

It left Vlod with a dull feeling, not in the pit of his stomach, but throughout his body. His hands tingled, and his feet went cold. He could feel the muscles across his shoulders and chest tightening, turn by turn, his own private rack.

Vlod had despised Morven, but now that he was dead, Vlod felt a profound sense of— What could he call it? Loss. It was loss. It wasn't grief, but loss, a lesser emotion, but no less powerful.

Voicing his deeper concern, Vlod asked, "How are the family?"

"As you'd expect," Ziellottes said.

The two men, one older and the other very much younger, stood in the hallway outside the classroom.

Ziellottes was a doer-of-deeds, a runner-of-errands, an excavator-of-facts, and a broker-of-information. He worked under the protection of one of the chieftains, but no one could find out which.

His ultimate employer's anonymity only served to amplify the impression of invulnerability that cloaked Ziellottes. As for his protector, because no one could puzzle out which chieftain it was, any of them could claim not to know who the man was, while at the same time dropping subtle hints, claims, that it was he. Which presupposed that any chieftain who did in fact have the information would be stupid enough to reveal that he did. Equally, any person who was intelligent enough to be Ziellottes' protector would also be intelligent enough never to reveal the fact.

And, in truth, it could be anyone. It need not be a chieftain. It could just as easily be a member of a chieftain's court, a wealthy merchant, a leader among the magi, an abbess, a châtelaine, or the Mother Metropolitan herself. Anyone!

Or no one at all.

Ziellottes himself had never—no, not once—claimed to be under anyone's protection. Indeed, he scoffed at the suggestion. Yes, he ridiculed it, but, as several people had observed, he ridiculed it without issuing an outright denial.

Ziellottes was that rarest of being: an honest spy.

The whole province knew damn good and well that he was a spy, but that meant that anyone could use his services without fear. He was everyone's friend, welcome anywhere and everywhere. Which meant that anything said to him in casual conversation might or might not be repeated, but most likely would be. He was a terrible gossip. In that sense, he was an open book.

But his openness, his transparency, also meant that any job he undertook and anything said to him in confidence was sacrosanct, never to be revealed and never to be repeated.

People, several people, had died trying to extract Ziellottes' secrets.

The sunlight streaming in through the windows had gone from bright to mocking. Wars—savage and ferocious campaigns—had begun with less cause than the killing of an heir.

But why had Wolfram sent Ziellottes? Why hadn't he sent an ordinary rider?

Because Wolfram also had some other task for Ziellottes to do, a task only Ziellottes could complete.

Vlod's questions spilled like grains of rice from a burst sack.

What task?

How was the household?

What was the state of play?

Were armies gathering?

Vlod decided to begin closer to the beginning. "How did it happen?" he asked, and began walking toward the nearest stairwell.

He was heading automatically out of the building and out onto open ground—open ground where they could be alone, open ground where they couldn't be approached without their knowing it, open ground where they could *see*, open ground where they could not be ambushed.

Ziellottes said, "The raid went sour."

That wasn't much of an answer.

Cattle raids weren't supposed to go sour. Their whole point was for them not to go sour. The objective was to trade a few punches, steal a few kisses from girls who were deep-down willing to have their kisses stolen, and run off with a few head. More often than not, the cattle were turned loose a klick or two away. "Against whom?"

"One of Vernon's settlements."

"Which one?"

"Eaufaulaton," Ziellottes said.

Morven could have picked a better target. Eaufaulaton was one of Clan Innes-Martin's so-called border-wall hamlets. In each hamlet, the barns and cottages were grouped behind a gated palisade. The palisade had an upper walkway that allowed archers to fire down on any attackers. Adding to the fun, Eaufaulaton was known to be inhabited by men-at-arms who liked farming, as opposed to the usual complement, which was farmers who could double as men-at-arms in a pinch.

"What happened? Who killed him?"

"Morven and his party struck as the cows were being led back into the hamlet for the night," Ziellottes said. "They had things in hand, and Vernon's people were giving as good as they got—the usual high spirits, but then there was an attack *in force* from inside the hamlet, by battle-hardened men-at-arms."

"Vernon's people were waiting for them?"

"That's Wolfram's guess."

"A trap, then?"

"Or heightened readiness," Ziellottes said. "This is the time of year for such stunts."

That was true enough. Spring and fall—after the rains have let up in the spring and between Mabon and the first hard frost in the fall—these were the seasons for cattle raiding.

"Normally such engagements are rough-and-tumble affairs," Ziellottes said, unnecessarily, "but this time it degenerated into a melee and the melee hardened into an all-out skirmish."

"For which Morven wasn't prepared."

"And from which he couldn't escape."

"They surrounded his force?"

"Yes."

"That's not part of the game," Vlod said, with an equal lack of necessity. Had the world gone mad? "The defenders *always* leave a way for the attackers to retreat. Their objective is to drive off, not kill."

"Not in this case. Vernon's people were out for blood."

By this time Vlod and Ziellottes had climbed up to a battlement on the up-slope side of the inner curtain wall. Above them, at no little distance on the other side of the cleared land, the trees stretched on up to the timberline. Above that sat an expanse of rock, fresh snow, and glaciers.

None of it was as solid as it appeared. The mountain was, in effect, a volcanic slag heap.

"How did he die?" Vlod asked.

They walked farther along the battlement. A cold gust boiled down from the summit, ruffling their clothes. It was one of the harbingers of the true fall, of the winter to come after it.

Ziellottes said, "The accounts vary, but the details amount to the same thing. Morven was sliced across the stomach, and when he bent over, he was decapitated." Ziellottes added, "One blow, clean, strong."

"Not the work of a frightened farmer," Vlod said. The conversation was taking too long. He was gnawing the details, like a dog going after a bone. "Were the blows left- or right-handed?"

Ziellottes shrugged. "I didn't see the body."

"What? They didn't ask you to examine it?" Vlod asked.

"No. Wolfram has asked me to prevent a war."

Vlod knew better than to ask, but he did, anyway. "How do you plan on doing that?"

Ziellottes treated Vlod to a sly smile. It made the spy look decades younger. "By delivering the news to you and then by pointing out to anyone who'll listen that war is a fickle mistress."

Vlod pivoted away from an exchange of aphorisms. He said, "I'll head back to Fort George immediately."

"Wolfram would rather you stayed here."

Vlod felt as though he'd been gut-punched.

"Morven—"

"By the time you get there, Morven will already be in his tomb."

What difference did that make? Vlod's place was with Edmund and his family, with his court.

"Wolfram was adamant," Ziellottes said. "You're to remain here. If Morven's death is part of a move against the Iredales, then you'd be an irresistible target, traveling alone."

"You're not headed back to Fort George?"

"No, I'm headed elsewhere. This chilly stop was on my way."

"I don't mean to preach," Vlod said, "but peace is an even more fickle mistress than war."

"That's the sort of thing Wolfram would say."

"I remain his faithful and obedient student," Vlod said.

"Peace is squandered by the peaceful."

"Who said that?"

"I did."

TWENTY-FOUR

Thora missed for a second year in a row. That made twenty-four months without a pregnancy.

It was a crying shame.

It was a tragedy.

It was the end of an era.

It always is, isn't it?

Well, she'd had a good long run, twenty-two years. Longer than most.

She'd started young, so her longevity in office didn't come as any surprise.

Where had the time gone? What had they accomplished in those twenty-two years?

Enough.

No, not nearly enough.

It could have been so much more.

The work is never finished. People come and go, but the work remains.

The work renews, like the moon and like the seasons. The tasks are never the same, but they are never different.

Like the moon.

Like the seasons.

The Wheel never stops turning.

And yet the Wheel remains.

How very pious of you, dear. I do so hope you can manage to be that sanguine when your time draws nigh.

Thora's court spoke aloud the thoughts that they had only whispered the year before. This made two years in a row, and two years in a row was a very long time. The crops were sure to fail. The fish runs were sure to be poor. The snowpack was sure to be thin. The Goddess was sure to withhold her favor.

I don't want to die.

The concerns are only metaphorical, dear. The granaries and the warehouses are bursting.

But—

Metaphorical. Do try to keep up.

Ulricka, Thora's friend and confidant, argued her cause. Duncan had been a pig. He had been a man of disgusting sexual desires, a man who stank of sweat and grease and excrement. It was no wonder Thora had had so little to do with him. As for Izanagi, the current year king, his seed had been weak and undeniably defective.

"How can you say such a terrible thing about him?"

"Because he's fathered three weaklings that have come to term. None of the Cathedral's women will have anything to do with him."

"You're making excuses!"

"I'm giving you explanations!"

Besides, Ulricka said, Thora was exhausted from work. There was trouble among the clans, upriver and down.

For example?

That unfortunate business with Morven.

Unfortunate? I say good riddance.

You can say whatever you wish. The Iredales and the Innes-Martins are at each other throats, and the Sauvies are teetering on the edge of being sucked into it.

I'm sorry they're having trouble, but they remind me of bats. I'm sorry, but it's true. They do, and if their troubles keep them out of our hair, so much the better.

Ulricka came close to giving her rage its head. Instead, she calmly pointed out that the situation was dire and that Thora could not risk turning her back on any of it. No, not for a single second.

Thora's personal physicians—a magus and a priestess, both of profound experience—argued that their mistress enjoyed robust health. True, she was no longer a girl, but they were certain that as soon as, shall we say, "conditions" righted themselves, she was bound to conceive.

The court refused to be silenced.

The clacking and the clicking in the passageways, the padding to and fro, the rasp of scales on marble floors, grew louder and louder.

Thora called a solemn assembly. Confronting her detractors, she again blamed her former consorts, especially Duncan, and begged their patience.

"The stench of him lingers," Thora said.

It must be an exceptionally powerful stench indeed.

When it came to Izanagi, her lack of enthusiasm was entirely understandable. Some seed never sprouts, and some sprouts but grows into twisted, misshapen things.

It was better for the entire province that she keep her distance.

The tide again changed and the skeptics again fell silent. As a whole, Thora's court was eager to be rallied to her cause. Thora was well liked, and no one wished to see her in the Grove.

Morven's War, as it came to be called, took light in an understandable firestorm of impassioned harangues. Vernon's and Edmund's armies moved toward their shared borders. Here and there, blows were exchanged, but the local field commanders held the fighting in check. They could not and would not risk attacking their opposite numbers without explicit orders to do so.

Ziellottes convinced Seldon, who was the third major chieftain on the lower river, to remain neutral, and he persuaded the Mother Metropolitan to stand back from the confrontation, to withhold moral condemnation of either side.

A cattle raid had turned nasty and people had been killed. Morven,

Edmund's heir, had been killed. It was cause for profound grief, but it was not a cause for the deaths of hundreds, if not thousands, of others. Cattle raiding is dangerous, and Morven had known the risks. Let it go at that.

"What of honor? What of justice? What of revenge? This cannot stand!"

"Where is the honor, the justice, or the revenge in the pointless death of innocents?"

"You sound like a monk!"

"Yes, and you sound like a man in the grip of a terrible loss. Your grief will never pass, but it will lessen."

"Never! They murdered him!"

"You cannot know that he was murdered. No one can. What we *know* is that he was killed in a raid, in combat. It wasn't supposed to have happened, but it did."

"You cannot assuage my anger with platitudes."

"Accepted, but let it be *your* anger. Do not let it become the personal *grief* of every Iredale household. If you do, they will rise up and turn against you. They will destroy you. And rightly so."

"Get out! Get out! Get out! You miserable jackal. When will you stop feeding on the dead and dying?"

The door closed, and he found the silence to be unbearable.

In the end, the chieftains who could remain aloof did so. The Mother Metropolitan called for peace and promised to punish any aggressors. Vernon backed away, and, finally, Edmund backed away.

But not entirely.

Rather than make war, Edmund built a wall. He fortified his border where it passed the closest to Vernon's lands. The centerpiece of this wall was a massive stone-and-timber gate. He named it for his dead son, for his murdered son. He named it Morven's Gate.

Ulricka discovered that she had an unsuspected love for the hunt. Hour upon hour of practice had made her good with a bow, and she wasn't the least bit squeamish about using it. She could dress her kills.

Above all else, she delighted in stalking her quarry, in the stealth and maneuver, in the deception and cunning needed to approach close enough to make a good shot, a killing shot, with her first arrow.

The use of a second embarrassed her, and the need for a third humiliated her.

TWENTY-FIVE

Vlod's senior year at the Academy began with a stint at the registrar's table. The weather was cold, overcast, and wet. The approach road was muddy, and the arrivals tracked the mud in through the main gate, across the cobbles of the outer ward, and into the registration tent.

Inside the tent, despite repeated trimming, the oil lamps refused to burn properly. They sent up noxious plumes of carbon-heavy smoke. The tent reeked of it, of damp wet wool, and of the horses beyond the door flap.

At the registrar's direction, Vlod made notes, catalogued confiscated items, ticked off names, and did his best to be friendly without appearing solicitous or, worse, unctuous.

There were a few late arrivals on the second day, and a handful of stragglers on the third.

On the evening of the third day, Master Yokashima sent an invitation to Vlod. Would he care to join his sensei for an evening coffee?

"Before the chaos begins, eh?" said Aerian, who'd stayed on for advanced studies in alchemy and engineering.

"I reject your premise, my friend," Vlod said. "The chaos is already upon us."

"Oh, so that's what you call them. A group of freshmen is a chaos. One freshman, two fresh*men*, and a chaos of freshmen."

"Why not?" Vlod said, trying not to remember that stream of bewildered, goggling, eager, stupid, embarrassed faces.

Master Yokashima lived in a second-floor suite above his dojo.

A spattering of low tables, reed mats, cupboards, and kanji wall hangings furnished the sitting room.

The old man who had nearly fought Vlod to a standstill in that long-ago interview, who could have had he chosen to do so, served the promised coffee. Vlod was again impressed with the length of the man's hands and the leather-bound queue hanging down his back. The boot knife the servant was wearing had an ivory handle and looked as though it had been handed down through countless generations. The servant bowed and withdrew.

The coffee's aroma hung over the table.

Yokashima took a long sip, and Vlod followed his sensei's lead.

"I honestly didn't think you'd survive your first year," Yokashima said.

"I remember," Vlod said, taking another sip of his coffee. "What's the reason I'm still alive?"

"The incompetence of the assassins she sends," Yokashima said, coming as close as he ever did to making a joke.

"I suspect a deeper cause."

"She had a change of heart."

Vlod knew better than to press the point. "Let's hope it stays changed."

"I believe it will. These days, she's preoccupied with other matters."

"Like what?"

"Her succession."

Vlod's vision tunneled down, and he felt a brief, intense touch of dizziness. "Succession?"

"She's approaching the upper limit for a mother metropolitan. Soon she'll no longer be able to have children."

"How can you be certain?"

"The calendar," Yokashima said. He smiled his sliest smile. "I have my sources, not that I need them. Nor a calendar. The routine dispatches have been enough. She has a year or two at most."

Vlod sighed.

"Is that relief I hear?" Yokashima asked. "Or is it satisfaction?"

"Both. I'm ashamed to admit it, but it's both."

"You'd be wise to keep such emotions on a tight leash," Yokashima said. "Thora is not the monster you believe her to be."

"She murdered—"

"By her lights, she executed an unrepentant heretic."

Vlod felt his jaws clamp tight.

"It's a hard truth for you to hear," Yokashima said, "but you must never underestimate her. You must never dismiss her as a power-mad, crazed tyrant. She is no such thing."

"Not from where I sit."

"Fair enough, but Thora's successor might well prove to be many times worse."

This was not idle speculation. Jumping down the rabbit hole, Vlod asked, "Really? How could she be any worse?"

"Well, for one thing, the new girl might learn how to hire competent assassins."

Vlod sighed, this time in recognition. "Now there's a pretty thought," he said.

At the Feast of Mabon, Qualicum lived up to the promise of his splendid muscle pack. He defeated Izanagi in a matter of seconds and dispatched every other challenger with a speed and an aplomb not seen in years.

The court knew Qualicum to be a man of powerful vitality and undoubted virility, as many a swollen belly among his chieftain's retinue attested. The geneticists would be working overtime to evaluate those pregnancies, to license them after the fact.

It was said that Qualicum was a man beyond restraint, but it was also said that he was unfeignedly considerate. He was strong and self-assured, no one's plaything, but neither was he a showy braggart.

The most promising of his attributes was that he was, beyond any conceivable doubt, highly skilled. He was, they said, as good a lover as he was a fighter, as good in bed as he was in the sacred arena.

Now that he was the new year king, he would, surely, perform what was needful for their beloved Mother Metropolitan—if she would but take him into her bed beyond the needs of ritual.

Beyond the needs of ritual.

And there lay the problem.

Her desire seemed to have evaporated.

Had she completely lost interest? Had her appetite dried up ahead of her body?

It was possible that it had, they agreed among themselves, and then they cast steady eyes upon the crops, the fish runs, and the mountain snowpack.

Well, whether she was interested or not, she had a duty to perform, didn't she?

She did, and Qualicum went to no small effort to spark her desire, to seduce her.

With varying degrees of success.

As if to confirm the Goddess' favor, by the Feast of Yule, Thora had conceived.

The Cathedral rejoiced, and Thora's court relaxed its undeclared vigils on the crops, the fish, and the snowpack. All was well.

For a time.

In the third month of her pregnancy, a few days after the Feast of Ostara, Thora miscarried. Given the nature of the feast, new beginnings and emerging life, the miscarriage was bitterly ironic.

Plainly, yet again, the Wheel had turned.

———

It was the coin of Thora's measure that without prompting, before the whispers and the rumors could take hold, at the conclusion of her morning audience two days after her loss, she called for her own succession.

Leaving them agape, she then retired to her private apartments.

Alone. With the doors locked. Not to pout, nor to grieve, but to rest, to gather herself for the struggle ahead.

When Thora announced her nomination of Ulricka to succeed her, they would not wish to accept her, but accept Ulricka they would, provided Thora could hold to the course she laid out for herself.

But she was tired. Worn out.

She threw those thoughts aside.

Self-pity wasn't like her, and she would not brook it.

Her determination, however, did not lessen her exhaustion, nor did it lessen the fact of it.

A woman of forty-three, she had reigned for twenty-two years and had *given*, as it was phrased, fourteen children to the Cathedral Henge of Eileen the Immortal.

Fourteen. Not a great number for so long a tenure, but adequate. The Goddess and the God had favored her.

Given? Each of those fourteen children had been stripped away from her as soon as it was decently possible. Each had been turned over to one or another of the nurseries to be raised as an anonymous Child of the Cathedral, to be raised among the streams of squalling infants produced by the girls serving their years in the Virgins' Pavilion.

Their *years*? They were hardly that.

The moment they conceived they were freed from the sexual aspects of the rite.

Thora never was.

The moment they delivered they were free to return home to their clans, their womanhood and their fecundity assured.

Some stayed for as little as nine months, conception to delivery. Others remained for as much as twenty-one months, conceiving only in the twelfth month of their residencies.

If they did not conceive within that twelve-month period, they were sent home, banned from the right and duty and joy to marry and bear children. They went home slated—some would say condemned—to perform other roles.

As for the Children of the Cathedral, a tiny minority of them stayed on at the Cathedral. They populated the offices, the clergy, the Guard, the Cathedral's river fleet. They worked in the fields and in the workshops. They tended the herds and they quarried the stone.

The majority, however, were distributed to the clans. There they were assigned to the manor henges in roles similar to those their siblings filled at the Cathedral, or they were taken into families that had fallen into childlessness, or they were apprenticed to one or another of the trades, or they were inducted directly into the clans' armies. Whatever the case, they were not wasted. They were not neglected.

Thora had nowhere to go, except to her grave. She was already *home*. She was not permitted to leave.

She was permitted to serve, to reign, to live as the temporal avatar of the eternal Goddess.

The Pavilion's graduates would marry, with any luck for love, and have families of their own. They would live with the same man, growing old together, until one or the other of them died—of accident, of disease, of old age.

Almost every year brought Thora a new consort, a new year king. One of them had lasted for four years, but most lasted for only one year —one bright, glittering, radiant, glory-filled, orgiastic year, and then they were dead, struck down by their successors, by the next year king.

Why did they do it? Why did they enter the arena to challenge the reigning year king?

Why had she agreed to accept nomination to become the province's Mother Metropolitan?

There were answers, but they were as absurd, as meaningless as the questions.

And as for *old* age? For living into her seventies or eighties, say? Or beyond? The thought of that made her laugh. She would never grow old. The Goddess is not, cannot be, a crone.

The graduates of the Pavilion would, in the main, raise their children into adulthood, and in the course of things, with the turning of the Wheel, they would help to raise their grandchildren. They would know them—as babies, as toddlers, as children, as adults. Now and then, sadly, they would bury them, mourn them, honor them. Always they would tell stories about them.

Thora never would. Her fourteen were unknown to her. It was

forbidden for her to ask what had become of them, who they were. Forbidden for them to know who their mother was, forbidden for them to ask, to seek. They were the beloved Children of the Cathedral, and nothing else. They had no heritage but the Cathedral, no parents but the Goddess and the God.

Twenty-two years.

And now it was nearly over.

Ended by a bloody mass of goo that might have grown into a baby, that might have grown but hadn't.

Twenty-Six

On the day after her announcement, Thora sent for Ulricka. Then on second thought, she sent for Shabnan, also. "Ask them to join me in the Terrace Room in two hours."

The attendant scurried out in a flutter of skirts.

With that task out of the way, Thora moved to her next task.

From the cedar chest in her bedchamber, where she had kept it, safely locked away against this very need, Thora retrieved the sword with which she had succeeded Alrys.

Throughout its many incarnations, the sword was named Rediviva.

Thora drew it from its scabbard, and for the first time in twenty-two years, she saw the gleaming steel.

The sword was cold to the touch, but precisely balanced, the handle textured to ensure a firm grip to a sweating, frightened hand.

Thora was no warrior, but she recognized an exceptional blade when she held one, and this, assuredly, was among the finest swords ever made, anywhere by anyone.

The light danced along its length, and the cutting edges and the crisp borders of the blood grooves threw off prisms of light, broadcasting the colors of the rainbow throughout the chamber. The colors of life. The colors of death. The colors of the turning of the Wheel.

"Hello, old friend," she said. "It is time."

She returned the sword to its scabbard and lay it on her bed.

Rediviva was not the only item the chest contained. There was also a bar of virgin steel, Victoria's Portion. The bar was about the size of a woman's hand and had been wrapped in an oiled, tightly woven wool cloth.

Thora unwrapped the bar. No rust had formed. Not a speck. It was the best of signs.

Alrys had shown her that very bar the morning of her succession, and had explained its significance. It was a reminder, a lesson in steel that the seasons never rest, but follow, one upon the other, inexorably. No matter your speed, no matter your care, no matter your strength, no matter your piety, you cannot outrun the Wheel. Nor should you.

Thora smiled at the memory, at how bitterly heavy the steel had felt in her hand then, at how terribly light it felt now.

She rewrapped the bar and tucked it into the belt of her dress.

She picked up the sword and left her apartments.

Walking alone, she made her way through the palace and across the inner courtyard, past the stables, past the smithy, with its aromas of coalsmoke, hot metal, and horses, and entered the Cathedral's armory.

The armory wasn't a large space, but it was open and had a high ceiling. Light streamed in through its expansive windows and skylights.

The forge held pride of place in the center, with a variety of anvils, vises, and water troughs positioned around it. A traditional leather bellows fed outside air into the forge, and a sheet-steel hood captured the fumes and smoke and directed them, via a chimney, out through the roof.

The armorer was sitting at a workbench. He was short and thick-bodied, large-boned, and had a laborer's muscle pack. He was well past middle age. He had thinning, nearly white hair, which he wore clipped short.

He was working on a man's ceremonial cuirass. It was a stunning piece: gleaming steel with gold and silver inlays, highly engraved. He was, or so Thora guessed, putting the finishing touches on the buckles.

He paused, turned, and saw her. His eyes widened, suggesting that he had also seen what she was carrying.

His face registered a wrenching sadness, but then widened into a welcoming smile. Rising to his feet, he said, "Vladika, what a pleasure it is to see you."

"And you," she said.

"How may I be of help?"

The question was a formality. He already knew how he was to be of service to her.

There was no escaping it, for either of them.

"You may re-forge Rediviva," she said, and delivered the sword and Victoria's Portion into his hands.

He permitted himself a brief public show of regret. "So soon?"

"The Wheel turns," she said.

"I'm not compelled to like it."

"No, you're not."

Using the ancient formula, Thora bid him to re-forge the blade, adding in the new steel, transforming the two of them into a new blade, which would also carry the name Rediviva, the blade that Ulricka would use to succeed Thora.

The armorer responded as the rite required, but then, still holding the blade and the bar in his work-hardened hands, he said, "It is the shame of the world."

"Thank you," she said, and removed a pendent from around her neck. It was silver, a gift from Ulricka. Handing it to him, she said, "Can you inlay this into the blade? I want my successor to be able to see it clearly."

It was a cardinal break with tradition, but then again, there had to have been a time when that tradition had been new. Let this gesture, this inlay, be the seed of a new aspect.

"It will be my pleasure to personalize the blade," he said.

She tried to respond but didn't trust her voice not to break.

His eyes on the point of brimming, he told her how he had been an armorer for forty years, how he had refashioned the metal that Alrys had used to succeed Katsu, how he had refashioned the metal that Thora had used to succeed Ayris, the very sword he was holding now, and how, above all, he had prayed to the Goddess that he would not live long enough to perform the service a third time. Katsu...Alrys...Thora...

"Who...?" he asked.

"Ulricka, if she'll have it."

"A wise choice, though it's hardly my place to say."

"Of course it is."

His face brightened. "The bowyers and the fletchers adore her. She's very good to them."

He began to cry openly.

She told him not to weep, but to consider the turning of the Wheel. "It breaks us all," she said, "but it also exalts us. It lifts us to the Gods and the Generations."

TWENTY-SEVEN

The Saraswati Palace was not a single building. It was several buildings. They abutted one another in a confusion of eras and styles and building materials. Stone towers and fully functional curtain walls, their battlements at the ready, snuggled next to glowering timber-and-plaster blocks, which in turn sat side-by-side with red-brick, utilitarian constructions. Square and octagonal log bastions rose high above flowing marble-clad villas that shone white and rose and pink in the sun. At night, they glistened, their colors muted, like mirages in the moonlight. Starlight was a special blessing to the villas. It softened them, caressing them as with a lover's touch.

It was one of these villas, graceful and open to the air, one of these delicate oases in stone, that housed the mother metropolitan's apartments, Thora's apartments.

They were a supple flow of rooms, sensible in their way, welcoming and comfortable. There was a summer room and a winter room, a breakfast room and a dining room, the Terrace Room, a study and a library, a sitting room and an audience room, a proper throne room and a game room, together with bedrooms, dressing rooms, privies, baths, offices, and servants' quarters.

But the palace was too cold, too austere, too filled with history, too decorated with the accumulated mementos of the past, handed down and enshrined.

Living in these apartments, Shabnan thought, would be like living in a mausoleum. She wondered how Thora, a very un-mausoleum sort of woman, had managed it.

Shabnan couldn't have done it, but then again, she had never tried. She had refused that jump. She had become instead the Crone of the Cathedral. She was the voice that whispered, the voice that jibed, the voice that spoke out, loyal but unafraid, the voice that would not be silenced. She was the voice that said what needed saying.

Why had she taken on such a role?

There was the power in it, yes, but that hadn't been the reason.

No, she'd taken it on out of her loyalty. Her devotion was to the metropolitanate itself, not to any particular mother metropolitan.

Alone in the Terrace Room, Shabnan waited, as she'd been instructed to wait.

The Terrace Room was Thora's favorite, her comfortable retreat, her fastness in the Cathedral's mountains of stone, timber, and brick.

The doors were closed, and the curtains dangled like corpses, hanging from a scaffold on execution day.

A polite knock, the door swung open, and Ulricka entered.

"Why has she sent for us?" she asked. Her voice was tight. Rather than sit down, she paced back and forth.

"She's called for her succession," Shabnan said. "Can't you guess why we're here?"

"No."

The child's mind had frozen. Panic so often rules when only clarity will do. Shabnan shrugged. "Then my efforts have been for naught."

"What are you saying? I don't understand."

The sharp tread of Thora's sandals sounded in the corridor.

"You will," Shabnan said, "and very soon now, I should say."

Thora entered the Terrace Room.

Her face was ashen, and her shoulders had rounded forward, drawing her upper body into a stoop. Exaggerating it, she was holding her head thrust forward, as though she were peering into a book.

With a twinge, Shabnan realized that Thora looked *old*.

It was her fatigue, surely. Yes, that had to be it. Thora wasn't old, not at her age.

Shabnan shuddered.

Denial.

It was a handy shield against the abhorrent, a weapon against inescapable necessities. It was like lighting a seven-wicked lamp in order to blind the wandering night spirits, as though spirits had physical eyes that could be blinded, as though they needed eyes to see, as though they cared about a pathetic wash of lamplight.

They didn't. Better to save the flint and steel. To save the wick and the oil.

Thora *was* old.

Thora looked directly into Ulricka's eyes. "I intend to nominate you to succeed me."

"You can't," Ulricka said. Her voice was unnaturally loud.

"I can, and I will," Thora said. "The questions is, will you stand for election?"

"No," Ulricka said. "I'm happy as I am. I have no wish to be the Mother Metropolitan."

"You're the only member of the Holy Synod who can be the Mother Metropolitan," Thora said. "You have the drive and the intellect and the youth."

"I do not."

"You do," Thora said. "I could nominate someone older, but she'd be dead before a decade was out."

Ulricka's face went from denial to terror.

"The Holy Tribunal for the Defense and Propagation of the Faith would never approve me," Ulricka said. "I was never an active priestess."

"They didn't object when I nominated you to become a châtelaine. If they balk, I'll insist."

"You won't have to, Vladika," Shabnan commented. "Besides, it wouldn't do you any good. Those self-righteous harpies can't be intimidated."

"I wouldn't count on that," Thora said. Continuing to Ulricka, she said, "The last thing this province needs is a caretaker."

"I don't have—"

"You'll have Shabnan," Thora said. "Others, too."

"You've been here your entire life," Shabnan said. "That ought to count for something."

"Your nomination can't come as much of a shock," Thora said. "What did you imagine we've been doing for these last months? These last years? Why do you think Shabnan and I have been showering you with attention and training and promotion? Did you imagine that we'd leave you to be another time-serving châtelaine?"

"No, I won't do it," Ulricka wailed. "Your successor must strike you down. I can't. I love you."

Very carefully, Thora said, "Which is why *you* must do it. Someone must. I'd rather it was you. A mother metropolitan may not be a crone. She is the vital avatar of the Goddess *as mother*."

"And life-giver," Shabnan said, completing the catechismal maxim.

"You could become the matriarch," Ulricka said, truly desperate.

"Her Holiness is not failing," Thora said. "She remains active and lucent. Her succession won't happen until long after I'm dead."

"Not necessarily," Ulricka said. "You could be consecrated as a living saint. The Cathedral Henge could nominate you."

The poor girl was grasping at straws.

It was time to snatch them away before they caused her to drown. Shabnan said, "Her Righteousness, the Most Venerable Thora, Servant of the Goddess and the God and Mother Metropolitan Emerita of the Inland Empire and the Holy Oregon. I like the sound of that. That's how you'd be styled, Vladika, once your nomination was approved. How grand!"

Thora arched an eyebrow at the Crone.

Undeterred, Shabnan said, "Better yet, that approval would keep you alive until Her Holiness decided what to do about you. That could take decades."

"That would be wonderful," Ulricka said.

Shabnan smiled her sweetest smile, but not for Thora. "Just think of it, Vladika, if you're canonized, they'd call you Her Sanctity, the All Blessed Thora, Holy among the Living." She shrugged. "Unless of course the old bat and her bootlickers decide against you. Then it'd be the axe and a simple-but-dignified funeral for you."

Ulricka's eyes were huge.

Addressing herself directly to Ulricka, Shabnan said, "I hear the odds are about one in a hundred of making it to the her-righteousness stage, and about one in ten of making it from there to the her-sanctity stage."

"Next you'll be telling me that there are a lot of simple-but-dignified funerals," Ulricka said.

"That's part of what she's telling you, yes," Thora said. "The canonization of a living person happens once in a generation. For a mother metropolitan to be approved for candidacy, let alone canonization? Perhaps twice in a century."

"We could—"

"Even if I were approved, the metropolitanate would fall vacant," Thora said. "I cannot continue in office. You must stand for election."

"No, I won't do it."

"You've already said that," Shabnan pointed out. It wasn't much of an observation, but she thought it might help to move the conversation along.

"You can and you will!" Thora said.

"I will not!"

Thora's eyes narrowed. She seized Ulricka by the wrist and dragged her into the Little Library, a book-lined reading room that opened off the Terrace Room. The door slammed with an ear-shattering report.

Shabnan sighed and went out onto the terrace, the terrace from which the room derived its name. She sat down in a comfortable chair and did her best to relax. Fretting would be of no use, but neither would pretending that everything was proceeding swimmingly and that they were in no danger.

As for danger, they were up to their necks in it.

Thora was right: now was *not* the time for a caretaker. If they ended up with one of those, the Province would succumb to Narmer's ambitions. Or to someone else's. The clans were ever restless. But Narmer, that megalomaniacal Egyptophile, was the odds-on favorite. He was smart and cunning, and he had a force greater than his power-lust driving him.

An exchange of shouts escaped the Little Library.

Shabnan had known that this was where the meeting would end up, and she also knew what the result would be.

She ought to have been a vision dancer…never mind that she couldn't keep time in an iron chest.

A dirge singer, then? Lose herself in the endless recitation of people's names, a recitation that ensured the immortality of those people.

The theology behind the *Dirge* mystified her. On the face of it, it undercut the omnipotence of the Goddess. The endless recitation of names. What was the ontological link between that and immortality with the Gods and the Generations? The Goddess was the supreme judge, the supreme arbiter of such things, was She not?

At the same time, Shabnan would have found the mildest challenge to that theology of the *Dirge*, to that practice, thoroughly abhorrent. She would have automatically reached for a bucket of pitch and a torch.

She made a face at the notion of her being a dirge singer.

She couldn't carry a tune, either, and she was too easily bored. Her mind would wander, and she'd make up stories about the people whose names she was reading. She'd become completely distracted. She'd lose her place, and that would never do.

The sun was pleasantly warm and the air was filled with the scents of the potted shrubs—pines of various sorts—and the scents of flowers—roses and bedding plants—and the chirping of large and small birds.

Just then, far, far overhead, off over toward the Cathedral Henge, an eagle cried.

The cry and its echoes reminded her of the day she'd taken Ulricka to visit the child's grave, Micah's grave, for that was the name that Thora had given him.

Shabnan closed her eyes.

She could hear Thora and Ulricka. They were still shouting at each other. The walls muted the sound, blurred the actual words, provided a measure of privacy.

She waited and tried not to listen.

After one especially vitriolic exchange, it occurred to Shabnan that it might be prudent to go back inside and stand guard outside the door to the Little Library. One or another of the servants might become alarmed—they were such a skittish bunch—and attempt to interfere.

That interference wouldn't do anyone any good: not Thora, not Ulricka, and most assuredly not the servant.

Shabnan returned to the Terrace Room and sat in a chair. It was a straight-back chair, very erect, very stylish, and very uncomfortable. Good. It would keep her awake.

A half hour passed.

Then another.

An hour and a quarter in total.

They sounded as though they might be winding down, as though their throats had been flayed beyond endurance.

Another quarter of an hour passed.

Now the shouting alternated with sobbing and silent periods. The levels rose and fell. Even the volume of the silence rose and fell.

A servant poked her head in from the corridor, but Shabnan waved her away. Run along, child. The grownups are busy.

Shabnan sent for a pot of coffee and a book. She drank the coffee and read. The book was a monograph on the theology of the *Dirge* and on the nature of memory eternal. At its base, beneath the pretty words, it was a book about death and the turning of the Wheel.

The coffee went cold.

She lost interest in the book—too many conditionals and too many metaphors confused with too many realities. What good was asking the right question if it, too, went unanswered?

The silence radiating from the Little Library relaxed into quiet.

The quiet absorbed time itself, but the Wheel did not stop.

As the sun was lowering and the light began to fail, the library door opened. First Ulricka and then Thora emerged. Their eyes were red and their faces were blotchy.

On the plus side, neither had scratched the other's eyes out.

Shabnan considered this a positive development. A mother metropolitan with one or both of her eyes missing might be bad for the metropolitanate's reputation.

Without speaking Ulricka left the room.

When her footfalls had faded, Shabnan asked, "Will she do it?"

"She's afraid of the blood," Thora said, "but, yes, she'll do it."

"There'll be quite a lot of it."

"I know," Thora said. Her voice was heavy with sarcasm.

"Oh, well," Shabnan said. "She's a hunter. She's seen blood before."

"This won't be like hunting."

"Maybe if you tied a set of antlers onto your head," Shabnan said helpfully.

"This isn't funny. She's terrified."

"I'll arrange some sort of training for her."

"That's your answer to everything, isn't it? Training."

"She cannot falter."

Thora looked out through the doors to the terrace, out across the terrace itself, out across to the Cathedral Henge.

"Neither can I," Thora said. "I wish I could drop dead."

Self-pity?

Well, what of it?

Thora was entitled to a measure of self-indulgence.

"What?" Shabnan asked, "And leave the Holy Synod to decide on its own?"

"They've managed before."

"They have," Shabnan said, "and consider the results."

She could recite the names of the mothers metropolitan who'd died suddenly—in childbirth, by disease, by accident, in war—and the names of the women who had succeeded them. Almost without exception, they'd been infamous disasters.

———

Shabnan's apartment, the traditional crone's apartment, was high on the southeast corner of the Saraswati Palace and provided an unobstructed view of the Cathedral Henge.

It was a gracious set of rooms, but in all honesty, Shabnan had more of them than she knew what to do with. Among them were antechambers, antechambers to the antechambers, a kitchen *and* a full-service pantry, a library *and* an office *and* a writing room, closets within closets, a breakfast room *and* a dining room.

The place was like an onion, peel away one layer and another was revealed.

Shortly after taking occupancy, Shabnan had done what she could to untangle the maze. She'd had walls moved, and she'd had walls removed.

Largely, she'd spent her own money, but in the end she'd had to call a halt and settle for what she'd been able to achieve.

Money hadn't been the issue. The stopper had come in the form of bearing walls and in the uncomfortable truth that she was the *temporary* occupant of an important and *historic* space.

The crone's apartment had a tradition of its own, and Shabnan believed that she had no right to demand changes that would undercut that tradition.

She could do what she could within that tradition, but she could not override it.

Nor did she have any serious desire to do so.

Despite her chaffing under its constraints from time to time, Shabnan believed that tradition was what kept people's feet on the ground. It ensured stability *and* it allowed for change. It enabled growth *and* it ensured against catastrophe. Tradition carried people through wars, plagues, floods, heresies, famines, and the deaths of mothers metropolitan.

Tradition had other uses, too.

Any hierarchy, for example, was purely a matter of tradition, as was obedience. Following right along, Shabnan felt that one of the traditional advantages of being an eminence, as opposed to a grace, was that she could summon Her Grace, the Right Reverend Ulricka, Châtelaine of Maupin and Warm Springs, with a politely worded invitation, rather than with a sternly worded command.

A short time after Shabnan had sent her politely worded invitation, the child arrived. Her eyes were red-rimmed and her face was blotchy.

Shabnan hoped against hope that Ulricka had already cried herself out and that she wouldn't discover fresh reserves of tears. She didn't seem the sort who would, but one could never trust appearances.

They sat in Shabnan's sitting room.

The cold leached from the stone of the walls and floors, but the fire on the hearth kept it in check.

Rather than tea or sherry, Shabnan poured them each a stiff drink of Spieden Blue, often nicknamed the Northern Fire. The liquor was pale blue in color and was one-hundred-and-twenty proof.

It wasn't sold by the case but by the bottle, each of which was witheringly expensive. Its contents were to be treasured and hoarded for occasions without parallel.

Shabnan hoped the child would not take Spieden Blue for an attempt to curry favor or to instill a comradery that did not and could not exist between them.

Ulricka sipped her drink, then drained away half of it.

"You asked to see me," Ulricka said.

Her voice sounded the way that peeling paint looks. It wasn't the Spieden Blue.

Shabnan drew in the aroma of the Spieden Blue, then sipped her drink. She thought how enjoyable it would be to become drunk on the Northern Fire merely by inhaling its aroma. It would be the alcohol fumes, of course, but *fumes* was too crude a word when it came to Spieden Blue. Besides, Shabnan wondered, was such a thing even possible?

Shabnan said, "Did Thora bully you into accepting?"

Ulricka thought before she answered. "No." She took a sip of her drink. "Thora can be a terrible bully, but, no, she didn't bully me. I didn't let her."

Now, there were words to hold onto in the days ahead. Shabnan refilled Ulricka's drink. "Why will you stand for election?"

"That, your eminence, is none of your business."

The armorer completed his work.

Thora set the new blade and the new Victoria's Portion aside and secretly buried Richland's Memorial in the Sacred Grove.

Each time Victoria's Portion was combined with the current sword, each time the new sword was fashioned, the total amount of steel was greater than that needed to form Rediviva's new incarnation. That excess steel was divided off, carefully set aside, and became Richland's Memorial.

It was like afterbirth—something that had been vital but that was no longer needed.

Thora couldn't quite remember why the excess was called Richland's Memorial, but she promised herself to ask Shabnan. She would know.

Holy Tribunal for the Defense and Propagation of the Faith questioned Ulricka, they examined her background, and they called in those who could testify to her character, morals, and faith. With a minimum display of handwringing they approved her nomination.

The Holy Synod fell into line and elected Ulricka to succeed Thora.

A few days later, the Congregation of Priestesses and Priests confirmed Ulricka's election.

It was done. All that remained was the doing of it, performing the actual rite.

TWENTY-EIGHT

As required by ancient practice and canon law, the Cathedral held a Tournament of Succession. At the end of a remarkably savage string of bouts, which left no fewer than a dozen combatants dead, Marquam faced off against Qualicum, the reigning year king.

The two men stood like statues, barely breathing, poised, on the knife edge of striking.

Silence gripped the area.

Time elongated.

It stretched out.

Then it hardened and turned brittle.

An eagle swooped and called.

The sound shattered Qualicum's focus, and he looked.

Marquam struck.

With a reverse cut, a stroke of such speed that few saw it, Marquam spilled Qualicum's guts onto the pumice of the arena. Qualicum fell to his knees and tried to stuff his intestines back into his body cavity, but they twisted out around his hands.

Marquam delivered the second of his blows without haste, and no one watching failed to see it, failed to appreciate its artistry.

Qualicum's head dropped, bounced, and rolled a short distance. Blood surged from the severed neck and spilled onto the pumice. The body collapsed into a trembling heap, but soon enough, the nerves stopped firing, and the body lay still.

The head gaped up at the sky, a look of incomprehension setting the features into an unforgettable mask. The eyes blinked.

It was almost as though Qualicum were conscious, but that had to be impossible.

The new year king finished by tossing his sword down onto his opponent's corpse.

Qualicum's face went slack, the eyes glazed.

It had lingered on for a few fractions of a second, but that was over.

The arena erupted in cheering.

Marquam waved to the wildly screaming throng and then strode from the arena.

The Dean of the Cathedral drew up and delivered the necessary announcement. It set the date for Ulricka's consecration.

Reading the document, written out in a clerk's neat, formal script, ink on parchment, the red wax seals bright, Thora was surprised to notice that she was barely able to hold the paper, barely able to lay it on her desk and affix her signature and seal to it.

"It's your death warrant," Shabnan said.

"No. I signed my own death warrant the instant I struck Alrys down."

"As you say," Shabnan said.

She took the document and handed it to an attendant. "Return this to the Dean. He's to post it as soon as practicable."

When the two of them were alone, Thora asked, "Will she be able to do it, do you think?"

"She's been practicing."

Thora's face paled. "On what?"

"Live deer. They're about the correct height."

"I'm not a deer."

"No, you're not."

"Well, then? Will she be able to do it? Cleanly. Without hesitation?"

"She has no choice."

TWENTY-NINE

I t's hard not to gloat," Vlod said.

His sensei, his mentor, Master Yokashima said, "About Thora?"

"Yes."

The practice field was empty now that the afternoon class had been dismissed.

The sky was blue, and a light breeze tumbled off the summit, cold from the snowfields.

"Joy in the misfortune of others," Yokashima said.

"It's an ugly emotion, and it's leaving me ashamed."

"As well it should," Yokashima said.

They walked, very slowly, toward the dojo.

The grass was rough and damp and cold under their bare feet, and Vlod could taste the snowfields on the air, like coastal rain, or blown sand, or the salt-laden air brought ashore by a storm.

"I need to talk to you about your father," Yokashima said.

"Go on," Vlod said. His shoulders tightened, and he had to make a conscious effort to relax them.

"It's time for you to hear one or two unpleasant truths about him, and after you graduate, it will be too late. Call it your final lesson in survival."

"I understand, Sensei," Vlod said, and forced his monkey mind to be still.

Yokashima sighed, almost as though he were profoundly embarrassed or profoundly grieved.

"You father was an arrogant fool. He would have done better had his attitude been one of humility."

Yokashima left a space.

Vlod refused to fill it. Back when he'd been a prickly freshman, excessively proud of his admission to the Academy, he would have screamed his defiance, his rejection of what his teacher and mentor was telling him, but now, the soon-to-be-graduating senior kept his face blank and his mind quiet.

He had anesthetized the monkeys, and that was how they were going to stay, even if he had to knock every damn one of them senseless.

"Thora executed him for heresy, but he left her no choice."

Was Yokashima making excuses for her?

"He would not hold his tongue. His pride wouldn't let him," Yokashima said. "She had to silence him, and that meant burning him at the stake."

"You're not excusing her, are you?"

"No, I'm explaining her actions." Yokashima's accent had thickened, as it did whenever he was experiencing a bout of inner turmoil. "You father, who was an honest and brilliant man, brought it on himself."

"How? What else could he have done?"

"He could have kept his results private. He could have shared them with trusted magi of like mind, men who were not likely to be overcome with jealousy or fear. He could have given the Cathedral time to formulate a response to what he had found. Instead, he pressed ahead heedlessly, publicly, and loudly. Proudly."

Another pause.

This time Vlod left his questions unasked.

Yokashima said, "You may hate me for saying so, but as I said, your father was fool. He could have lived. He could have prevailed. He could have gone on with his research. But he chose to throw his life away on a public display. It was the very height of hubris."

The monkeys shrieked into wakefulness. They chittered and howled. They bounded from tree limb to tree limb, pointing and screaming and laughing.

Vlod confined himself to, "I can't forgive her."

"I'm not asking you to. It's much too raw.

"And, please, don't hand me the speech about the two graves."

"Never. But I am asking you to not judge her with needless severity. She had reasons for what she did, and your father may as well have lit his pyre himself."

The monkeys...the crippling bedlam of their noise. It stabbed into Vlod's mind, into his very essence. Thora had no need to assassinate him. He was doing it on her behalf.

Two graves, and no mistake.

Yokashima said, "Thora was perfectly correct, intellectually."

The quiet of his words broke through Vlod's inner uproar, sundering it.

"The fact that your father could not find the ash does not prove that it does not exist. It proves only that *he* could not find it." Yet another pause, and then, "He fell into one of the common logic traps, and it cost him his life."

THIRTY

The appointed day for Ulricka's consecration dawned bright and sunny. Puffy clouds fleeced the blue sky, and a chorus of breezes danced and whirled between the monoliths of the Cathedral Henge of Eileen the Immortal.

Looking up at the sky, Shabnan said, "It would be interesting to be able to read them, those clouds, as though they were vision dancers."

"Worried?" Thora asked.

"I'd rather not be."

"She'll have you at her side."

"If she'll listen."

"You're hard to ignore."

"She might turn me out to grass."

"She would be damning herself," Thora said. "By the way, why is it called Richland's Memorial?"

"The sword that became Rediviva originally belonged to Richland. He had seized it from his father and struck him down with it."

Thora remembered then. Her knowledge of the history cut through her gathering terror, her incapacitating sense of what lay ahead.

How long?

Not long.

Soon it would be over.

Shabnan was saying, "Victoria seized it and used it to strike down Richland, thus establishing the succession of the mothers metropolitan."

Out of sight from where they stood, a priestess struck the hour on a massive gong.

"Thank you, Shabnan," Thora said. "Thank you for everything."

"Vladika, you have brought great honor and blessing to the Cathedral Henge of Eileen the Immortal."

The members of the General Convocation of the Province of the Inland Empire and the Holy Oregon processioned into the innermost circle of the Cathedral Henge, the Sacred Klickitat Ring. They had come from across the Province, from each of the manor henges, and from the Province's religious communities, temples, and shrines. Also in attendance were representatives from several of the bordering provinces.

The congregants filled the Sacred Klickitat and then the rest of the Henge, and when the Henge was full, they overflowed across the expanse of the mount. Like a living flood, they spilled down the Pilgrim Road and past the Wall of the Year Kings.

The sun brightened the colors of their robes.

The air bore the scents of their various perfumes.

The Dean of the Cathedral opened the Rite: "Goddess sanctify!"

"So and blessed let it be!"

A lengthy set of prayers followed. The words echoed between the monoliths.

A series of questions and antiphonal assents came next, and then, too soon, too abruptly, the ritual dialogue ended, and the Cathedral Henge went silent. No one stirred. No one shuffled their feet. No one coughed.

The one sound to be heard, the one sound that Thora heard, was the fluttering of the ceremonial torches.

Acting in her role as Crone of the Cathedral, Shabnan nodded to Thora and Ulricka.

Their faces grave, the two women, spent old age and overflowing youth, stepped into the center of the Klickitat Ring.

Shabnan brought out the reforged blade and the bar of newly smelted, newly forged steel. Flanked by two priestesses, she carried them on a sky-blue cushion and conveyed them toward the Mother Metropolitan and the Mother Metropolitan-Elect.

Despite hours and hours of practice, Shabnan was fearful that at any moment she would trip, or lose her balance, or allow her grief to overwhelm her, that she would stumble and drop the sword and the newly forged steel, that the strength of her arms would give out. That she would lose her self-control, decry the rite, renounce her faith, and flee the Cathedral Henge, that she would curse the Goddess for a blind, unthinking, capricious, and merciless tyrant.

That night in the Grove when they had buried Micah she very nearly had.

She was thankful that the day was bright, that she could see the pavement clearly.

The soles of her sandals rustled on the paving stones. Sweat trickled down her back, and her eyes stung.

She must be crying.

What a gauche thing to do, now of all times.

How vile this method of succession was!

How repugnant! How barbaric! How primal!

How necessary!

The words screamed themselves in her mind.

She silenced them and surrendered herself to the rite. She had a sacred role to play, and play it she would. To hell with her doubts and her emotions.

Shabnan and the two priestesses came to a stop in front of Thora and held out the sword, sheathed in its shining ebony scabbard, together with the bar of new steel. The scabbard was as new as the sword it housed.

Thora accepted them with a formal bow, leaving the cushion empty in Shabnan's hands.

One of the priestesses took away the cushion, and then the two priestesses retired.

Shabnan, the Crone of the Cathedral, went to her place, her new place, at Ulricka's side.

Thora offered the sword and the bar of new steel to Ulricka, who accepted them.

She looked terrified.

She had every right to. In accepting election, in accepting her consecration, she had condemned herself.

Ulricka passed Victoria's Portion to Shabnan and stepped forward into the center of the inner ring, carrying the sword, sheathed in its scabbard.

Ulricka asked the next series of questions in the rite, and the members of the Convocation answered them.

The final question was, "Is it your will and bond that I serve you and the Goddess, the God, and the Generations as your Mother Metropolitan?"

"It is!"

Thora's voice rose above the rest.

"Goddess sanctify!" Ulricka said, her voice clear and strong and choked at the same time.

She might make it through to the end without faltering. She just might do it.

"So and blessed let it be!" came the antiphonal response from the Convocation.

Then, with the echoes of the acclamation sounding from stone to stone, with a corps of breezes dancing among the monoliths, weaving in and out, twirling and leaping, Ulricka drew the sword.

The sunlight shone along the newly forged blade, Rediviva. The light, clear and strong, glinted along the cutting edges.

Ulricka handed the scabbard to Shabnan, who took it and stepped away.

Ulricka and Thora faced each other.

The Sibyl of the Cathedral edged closer. Her view must not be obstructed.

The sword's handle was rough in Ulricka's hand. She resettled her grip, working her flesh into the handle's texture.

Now they would see the result of her training.

Ulricka must strike as the way-master had taught her to strike, strike as she had struck the bamboo, the target dummies, and the living deer they had provided. Again and again, she had struck, deer after deer, until both she and the way-master were satisfied with her skill.

The butchers, no doubt, had blessed her.

She must not slip; she must not shrink; she must not falter; she must not turn away. She must empty her mind!

Thora's eyes were clear, her head high, her mouth firm.

Ulricka placed her feet, securing them on the paving stones.

Again she settled her grip on the sword's handle. She lifted the terrible blade, the ancient reforged blade, the new blade, *her* blade, fashioned from ancient steel, lifted it as the way-master had taught her, as had become instinctive, automatic. She held it high, two handed, the steel above her right shoulder, slanted upward.

With the weight of the weapon solid in her hands, she sought courage in the one place where she might find it: not in the approbation of the Convocation, not in Thora's eyes, not in her own determination, not in the divine love and will of the Goddess and the God, not in the cleansing of her mind of deliberate thought, but, as Shabnan had taught her, in the sweep of time, in the traces of the Wheel, in the Wheel's own turning.

Even the Goddess and the God might pass from existence, might die, just as people died, but the Wheel would remain, turning, forever turning.

Long, long ago, the people forgot and turned away.

But the Goddess bided her time.

Century after century.

Then, a scant seven centuries ago, when the earth could endure the mindlessness and the evil no longer, the Goddess sent Her devouring thunder.

It was an act of kindness.

The shatterers fell, the incarnations of Shiva and Kali. The high, proud cities and the gloating demons within them burned.

Their ash, black and thick and stinking, filled the skies and covered the land. They blotted out the sun.

The Goddess in Her love for humanity caused the Great Winter to descend. It cleansed the earth and prepared the path...if Her people would but set their feet upon it.

They refused. They mourned their old ways and longed to return to them.

A generation passed.

The Goddess waited, patient and unafraid.

A second, and then a third generation came and went.

Still She waited, aloof but watching, weeping with Her people in their distress, laughing at their efforts to rebuild the monstrosity.

It was the fourth generation that remembered Her.

They opened their crusted eyes, and raised their parched voices and lifted their emaciated hands. They called to Her out of the freezing darkness and out of their despair.

She heard them and She took pity on them.

She drowned the black skies in the light of the sun, the moon, and the stars. The rain fell bright and pure. The snows were no longer gray. The air no longer smelled of soot and ash and burning oil.

The people saw, as though for the first time, the Wheel and the Wheel's turning, and they rejoiced.

It was the first year of the Second Creation, and Vancouver ruled over the people, and the Goddess welcomed them home.

After all that had happened, however, the Goddess demanded a heavy price, one not immediately revealed, but one to be exacted without pity. The people must not forget; they must not return to the old ways. The price would teach them to remember.

The years flowed in quiet succession.

Vancouver restored the worship of the Goddess. He planted the first oaks in the Sacred Grove, and he sent forth messengers and prophets. Henges dotted the Inland Empire and the Holy Oregon.

The people were happy, and the crops grew abundantly.

But the Wheel never stops.

By the third decade of Vancouver's reign, gray had filled his beard, his back had bent, and his eyes had turned watery. He hunted less, and his wives complained of his inattention.

The crops withered, famine overtook the land, and the people suffered.

The price was due to be paid.

Richland, Vancouver and Attalia's oldest boy, came forward and paid it.

He stole his father's sword and in single combat, struck him down with it.

The people blessed Richland and buried Vancouver in the Sacred Grove because they mourned him.

Richland, however, was a child in a man's body. He was not his father.

Richland fought many wars, both for glory and for conquest. He sought the things of old: the old ways, and the old ambitions, and the old sources of wealth. He rediscovered the past, and he clung to it.

No one opposed him, and it appeared that the people had again forgotten.

The crops failed, and famine plagued the land.

But then Victoria, a priestess of the Goddess and the God, seized Richland's sword, the very sword that he had stolen from his father, and in single combat, she slew him with it.

The people blessed Victoria and buried Richland in the Sacred Grove. They did not mourn him, and they did not honor him. They buried him in the Sacred Grove because it was his due, despite his sins.

They returned his possessions, the old things, the curiosities that he had dug up, to the ground. They smashed the inventions and the rein-ventions that he had made. They emptied the libraries and burned the books that had survived the Great Winter.

Such knowledge was a danger to the people and an affront to the Goddess. It was a pure and malignant evil.

Victoria put the sword away and ruled over the people. She ruled with compassion and grace and beauty. She took a consort and had many children by him, and the people were happy and the crops did not fail.

The years passed, and Victoria grew old beyond her years. She was loved, but as she weakened, the crops weakened. Each year brought fewer bushels than the last.

Acting upon a sacred vision, she conveyed the Sword of Vancouver and a bar of virgin steel to the armorer. She commanded him to reforge the blade, using the old blade and the virgin steel.

He added the virgin steel to the blade and removed a similar amount of metal. That extra metal, combined with the dross and the slag from the forging and engraving, he placed in a leather bag.

The armorer delivered the finished sword, a new piece of virgin steel, and the bag of excess metal to Victoria.

She took the sword and named it Rediviva, because it had been reborn, revivified.

She referred to the bag, only half seriously, as Richland's Memorial, but the name stuck. Acting alone, she buried the bag in a secret place, returning it and its contents to the earth, completing their cycle.

At the appointed hour, Victoria bestowed the new sword and the piece of virgin steel upon Charlotte, and Charlotte used the sword to strike down Victoria.

Charlotte understood the significance of the virgin steel.

The Wheel never rests, and yet the Wheel never changes.

The people hailed Charlotte and buried Victoria in the Sacred Grove. They tore their garments.

When it was Charlotte's time, she delivered the sword and the bar of virgin steel, which she called Victoria's portion, to the armorer.

When the armorer had completed his work, he gave the sword, Richland's Memorial, and the new Victoria's portion to Charlotte.

In a place unknown to anyone but she, she buried Richland's Memorial. The reforged blade and the new Victoria's portion she bestowed upon Georgia.

And Charlotte was followed by Georgia...and a new year king, Gilford, a mighty victor, was crowned...

And in time, Georgia was followed by Quenelle...

And the Cathedral Henge of Eileen the Immortal was built on the northern shore of the Columbia River...

And Quenelle was followed by Hope, and Hope was followed by Marcellina . . .

The Cathedral's Holy Tribunal for the Defense and Propagation of the Faith declared Vancouver to be the first year king.

Vancouver was disinterred and reinterred in the Wall of the Year Kings.

Several months later, Richland, too, was reinterred in the Wall, but with much less fanfare and ceremony.

And so it went, on and on, down the generations, until the nomination and the election fell to Katsu, who was followed by Alrys, who was followed by Thora.

And here Ulricka reached the end.

But not quite.

She must not shrink. She forced herself to remember. She calmed her mind. She persuaded it now to have no thought, no past, no future, and no present.

The Wheel turned and Ulricka struck.

The ancient steel, Vancouver's sword, as sharp as art could make it, sliced into the base of Thora's neck, where it rounded into her left shoulder. The blade went deep, nearly severing the spinal cord.

The blood sprayed up, all the more when Ulricka pulled the blade free.

Thora's eyes were wide in shock, in surprise, in pain. Her mouth opened to scream, but no sound beyond a blood-soaked cough emerged.

She clutched at the wound as she fell.

Thora's body collapsed onto the paving stones. The blood spread across them, red and bright in the sunlight.

Her Beatitude, the Most Blessed Ulricka, Mother Metropolitan of the Inland Empire and the Holy Oregon, did not turn away. She did not weep, she did not howl, she did not scream out against what she had done.

The Sibyl rushed forward to read the throes. Thora's blood drenched her skirts.

The body thrashed and twitched and convulsed.

And still Thora made no sound beyond a choking moan.

The stench of a slaughterhouse filled the Klickitat Ring.

Thora twisted, arching her back, clutching at the base of her neck.

Then she stiffened, and rattled, and it was over.

She was dead.

Her blank eyes stared upward, upward at Ulricka, returning the new Mother Metropolitan's stunned, frightened gaze.

The Sibyl circled the body several times. Her head cocked first to one side and then to the other, as though she were listening, as though she were expecting something further.

The stench intensified.

Shabnan handed Ulricka a cloth.

Ulricka used it to clean the blade. She left behind no trace of Thora's blood. She held the sword aloft.

"So and blessed let it be!" she intoned.

The Sibyl announced the augury of Thora's death: good fortune and a long and fruitful time in office for Mother Metropolitan Ulricka, many daughters and sons.

Ulricka sheathed the sword, Vancouver's sword, Thora's sword, her sword.

The cheers went up, and later, after the feasting, Ulricka went in to her consort, Marquam, her first year king.

Ulricka made him hers, and together they announced that she had done so, just as the Rites of Consecration required.

The people blessed Ulricka, and they buried Thora in the Sacred Grove. They tore their garments and they planted an oak tree in her name.

Later that same night, Ulricka bathed alone. She had neither her attendants nor her consort with her. Alone she padded through the Mother Metropolitan's apartments, her apartments.

She knew them intimately—the coldest alcove in winter, the best window to catch a breeze in summer, the best place to find solitude. Tonight, however, the rooms, the Terrace Room, the summer room, the winter room, the audience room, and the rest, seemed strange and frightening. Rather than embracing her, they surrounded and enclosed her. They ensnared her, and they imprisoned her, and in time, they would consume her.

She recognized the walls, the floors, and the doorways, but they had removed Thora's objects, her hangings, and her ornaments, even the ones that had been gifts from Ulricka.

The apartments were anonymous and frozen, as dead and impersonal as they must have been when the very first mother metropolitan to occupy them had moved in.

Ulricka thought about who it must have been. She worked her memory until she had the name: Fiona. Fiona had been the first to occupy these rooms.

How many years ago?

Ulricka refused that jump.

Centuries.

How many?

Never mind how many. Centuries.

She left it at that.

She padded into the mother metropolitan's private bedroom, and she considered the mother metropolitan's bed, entirely new, a bed of her choosing, installed during her Consecration.

The bed had been freshly made and the room had been freshly redecorated for her, as she had specified.

To her surprise, on the nightstand she found a note from Thora, its blue wax seals unbroken.

Ulricka broke the seals and read. Thora had written to beg her forgiveness for nominating her, to beg her forgiveness for having been weak and selfish, to wish her the boundless courage she would need, to wish her well in office, a blessed tenure, and to bestow upon her the blessings of the Goddess and the God.

Ulricka read the note through a second time, refolded it, and closed it in the drawer of a dresser, a dresser of her choosing, installed during her Consecration.

Alone she cried for Thora, and alone she cried for herself, and alone she went to sleep.

The Wheel turned.

Thirty-One

That same year, at the summer solstice, at the Feast of Litha, in the first year of Ulricka's reign, Vlod graduated from the Academy of Archmagus Basil the Anchorite and Wonderworker.

After a further round of examinations and interviews, he was duly enrolled in the Guild of Augurs, Seers, and Soothsayers.

As Edmund had promised, and contrary to the common practice, the College of Magi assigned Vlod to Clan Iredale.

He was going home.

His work, his true work, was about to begin.

Where was the ash?

Turn the page for a preview chapter of the next book in The Assassins of Harmony series, *Ulricka's Gambit.*

ONE

A strident knocking rattled the door to the Mother Metropolitan's sitting room in the Saraswati Palace.

Her Beatitude, the Most Blessed Ulricka, Mother Metropolitan of the Inland Empire and the Holy Oregon, now in the fifth year of her reign, looked up from the Senet game she was about to lose to Her Eminence, the Most Reverend Shabnan, Crone of the Cathedral Henge of Eileen the Immortal.

The two women's eyes met in anxious anticipation.

Was this, finally, the news they had been waiting for?

No one but an officer of the Cathedral guard would dare to hammer in such a manner, and no one but an officer of the Cathedral guard could be entrusted to deliver such an important message.

Surely, this could not be another report of failure, not at this absurd hour.

Throughout the evening and deep into the night, one after another, the messengers had announced the near misses or the catastrophes in the guard's hunt for one old priest. Was another such announcement about to be dropped into Ulricka's lap, or would this be the message that Ulricka had been praying for?

"Come!" she said. Her voice reflected her twenty-eight years of life, her five years in office, and her four successful pregnancies—four babies carried to term and thus four children bestowed upon the Cathedral. Her tone was reflexively determined, accustomed to command and certain of obedience.

The door swung open, and an officer entered.

A figure loomed in the passage behind her, excluded and blocked. She was a runner, an adolescent in a woman's uniform. If all went well, she might live long enough to grow into it.

The runner dodged around the officer and bolted into the room.

The girl was all arms, legs, and excited eyes. She reeked of grime and sweat. She was menstruating, too, and the rotten-fish stench of it simmered beneath the rest. She'd have to change her pad soon or she'd stain her kilt.

Given the recurrent, heretical itch to reinvent lost technologies, or to make up new ones, why was it that no one ever sought to reintroduce cotton pads or, better still, tampons?

Perhaps it was because those who did march to that drummer had other things on their childish minds.

Currently, rumor had it that one of the downriver magi had taken it into his head to figure out a way to harness horses to a capstan, much as it was done in sawmills and flour mills, and then use the power generated to drive the wheels of a wagon or to turn a set of paddlewheels on a boat.

What was the point? Horses pulled, rowers rowed, and sails propelled. Anything else threatened the Harmony.

The runner bowed.

Why was it always things like self-propelled wagons and boats with neither sails nor oars? Why not looms and lumber mills and, for the sake of argument, machines to dip candles?

The runner came to attention.

Ulricka answered her own question: no cheap cotton. The Columbia River Basin had a temperate climate, and because it did, cotton couldn't be grown locally, not in any commercially viable volume. Cotton had to be brought in overland by caravan. Therefore, cotton was an expensive luxury.

As for raising it elsewhere on the continent, the volume of labor needed to grow it in commercially viable amounts simply didn't exist. And that was *before* considering the additional amount of labor that would be needed to process the raw cotton into useable products, like cloth, pads, tampons, and summer-weight garments.

The runner stood mute, her eyes fixed on the wall behind Ulricka.

A routine intelligence report had mention—in passing, for the love of heaven!—that Vlod of the Iredales was trying to use the pressure of steam to push water through a pipe.

Steam as a motive force! It was nothing but an invitation to heresy, upheaval, and death.

Thora, the previous mother metropolitan, ought to have done away with that runt years ago, but she'd missed her chance, and her subsequent, half-hearted attempts had been bungled affairs at best.

Well, Ulricka thought, what hadn't been done might still be done. Like his father, the runt might even be persuaded to light his own pyre.

Why didn't the runner speak? Was she waiting for permission?

No, she couldn't be that silly, not on a night like this.

Then again, maybe she could be.

Deciding to rescue the poor child, Ulricka asked, "What do you have to tell me?"

The runner caught her breath, then blurted, "Your Beatitude, Colonel Chiharu sends her devotion. She is pleased to inform Your Beatitude that the traitor Jinhai has been found in the Sacred Grove."

The words had spilled out in a jumble, like a dozen kittens being dumped from a wicker basket.

Ulricka and Shabnan shared a look of triumph.

"May the Goddess bless Colonel Chiharu," Ulricka said. "She is not to break contact but neither is she to capture him. I shall join her shortly."

"Yes, Your Beatitude," the runner said. She bowed and hurried out.

The officer followed, but at a dignified pace.

The door closed with a sharp click.

Ulricka swirled her winter cloak across her shoulders and closed the clasp. She hooked a quiver of arrows onto her belt and picked up her favorite bow, the laminated recurve she used to hunt elk.

A gentle delight in the foibles of youth flared in Shabnan's eyes.

"You are Dianna in the flesh," she said.

"Don't blaspheme. We shall need Her blessing."

"No disrespect was intended." Shabnan reached for her own cloak. "Will you murder him?"

"I must," Ulricka said. "Both him and his handlers. The Cathedral's safety depends upon it."

Shabnan cocked her head to one side. Deciding to speak, she said, "Yours too."

"I'm a cipher," Ulricka said.

Shabnan shrugged. "What about the baby you're carrying?"

Ulricka's hands went cold. "How did you know I'm pregnant? I've barely just figured it out myself."

"I am the Crone of your Cathedral. How could I not know? Your court will rejoice."

"They aren't the ones who'll have to bring it to term and then deliver it."

"Hence their great joy. Other women's babies are such a delight, don't you think?"

Shabnan opened a drawer in the base of the Senet board and moved to sweep the pieces into it.

"Don't," Ulricka said. "I'd like to finish that game."

"You can't possibly win."

"I have my hopes."

His Honor, the Venerable Jinhai, Archdeacon, Protopriest, and Archthurifer of the Cathedral Henge of Eileen the Immortal, ran south through the Sacred Grove. The ancient oaks stood thick on the ground, and he found that he had to dodge between them.

It reminded him of playing soccer in his youth, of moving the ball down the field. He would pivot and dart this way and that, risking his knees and his ankles, and all in an effort to avoid the players on the other team, in a desperate drive to get close enough to the goal to kick the ball past the goalie and into the net.

The roots of the trees bulged beneath the grass. They made it dangerous for him to run in the dark, but he had no choice. He would either make his rendezvous or he would die.

A wall loomed up sixty meters ahead of him. Made out of rough stone, it was less than a meter-and-a-half high. It was a demarcation rather than a barrier, like a decorative railing on the edge of a scenic clifftop.

Beyond the wall sprawled Maryhill, the city that served the Cathedral and its precincts.

If Jinhai could make it over that wall, if he could accomplish that much, then he might be able to disappear into the town's warren of streets and alleys. There, he might be able to elude Chiharu, and having eluded her, he might—May the Gods and the Generations grant it!—be able to reach the Columbia River and rendezvous with Ziellottes, his handler.

Jinhai had only one purpose: to warn the clans about Ulricka! The Cathedral, no, the entire province, hung in the balance.

His right boot came down wrong and slipped on the wet grass. Jinhai stumbled, nearly falling, but he regained his footing and plunged on into the night, on into the shadowed maze.

Just then an arrow struck one of the oaks, ahead and slightly to the left. It had missed by less than a quarter of a meter.

He recognized the gold-and-purple fletching. Ulricka had joined the hunt!

Had she shot wide deliberately?

No, not Ricki. She'd missed.

Jinhai stole a glance back. His pursuers were gray-black shapes, as silent and as quick as wolves, coming on among the trees.

Looking back on what had happened, Jinhai decided that the crisis had begun two days earlier. It had sprung like a slow-moving bear trap.

The senior librarian had informed him that he had been unable to locate the book that Jinhai had asked him to bring up from the closed stacks.

The book in question was *The Council Crest Grimoire*. It wasn't a terribly important book, but Jinhai had wanted it to clear up one or two points in his current research. That research was into the influence, if any, of the cave cults and mountain covens on the early origins of the Cathedral's present-day liturgical practices. Had there been carryovers, and, if so, what was their meaning, recognized or otherwise?

The librarian's failure to locate a requested volume was not in the least unusual. Library staff often returned volumes to the wrong shelf.

However, *The Council Crest Grimoire* was not a popular volume. Indeed, as far as Jinhai was aware, he was the only researcher who had any interest in it. Thus the staff would have had little or no opportunity to misshelve it since the last time Jinhai had accessed it.

The book, logically speaking, ought to have been in its correct place on the correct shelf, rather than in the wrong place on the wrong shelf.

Stranger still, the librarian had not offered to conduct a search for the book. Moreover, he had flatly refused to grant Jinhai access to the closed stacks in order to search for it for himself. It was an unheard-of slight to a senior member of the Cathedral's clergy.

Yesterday one of the junior thurifers had failed to appear for a mandatory rehearsal. She had sent no note of explanation, no request to be excused, and no apology.

Under normal circumstances, such behavior might well have resulted in her dismissal, and she would have had to have known that it might; nevertheless, she had dared to do it.

Then, at midmorning today, Howahkan, another of the Cathedral's protopriests, had sent word that an unavoidable conflict had arisen, forcing him to cancel their working lunch.

Their working lunches were nothing of the sort. Rather, they were once weekly times when they could gossip for a couple of hours, all the while eating and drinking as they never did otherwise.

Over the years, Jinhai had found it necessary to cancel two or perhaps three times—he couldn't remember exactly—but Howahkan never had. Never! If he had died the day before, his corpse would have kept the appointment.

And yet, he had sent his excuses.

Significantly, Howahkan had not suggested another time.

As Jinhai had thrown Howahkan's note into the stove in his apartment, his mind engaged what appeared to be a growing threat.

Had he put his foot into a trap? Had he put his weight on the pressure plate? Were those the sounds of the jaws swinging closed?

Perhaps.

Taken individually, the events were meaningless. However, taken as a group, they forced an inescapable conclusion. The Cathedral guard were asking questions and dropping hints. They were isolating Jinhai from his colleagues. Doubtless, they had already begun to demonize him. They were making him a target for arrest, for the stake.

But if their intent was to arrest him, why hadn't they? Why the cat-and-mouse games?

That wasn't much of a question. They wanted to know how much he'd revealed. They wanted to snap him up with his hands dirty. They wanted him to lead them to his contacts, to snap them up as well.

That being the case, their only choice was to play him on a long line. But they had both waited too long and had moved in too quickly.

It was understandable. The situation was both fluid and murky. It was like hunting carp with a bow and arrow. Easy enough to do in clear lake water, but when the river's shallows were muddy and the fish had gone deep, success was largely a matter of luck.

Jinhai had not been so silly as to believe he could evade them indefinitely, but neither had he expected them to discover him so soon.

The last of Howahkan's note collapsed into the flames, like the final parts of a heretic's burning corpse.

Jinhai took several deep breaths and recited a calming mantra. This was not a convenient time to panic.

He reasoned that the guard would not be ready to strike for several more hours, perhaps not until dawn.

Dawn was a good time for such goings-on.

And, too, despite their lust for heroics, they were a sluggish lot.

No, all in all, he had ample time. The wood wasn't piled around his legs just yet.

He coded what would of necessity be his final report. He finished with an urgent request for extraction and a promise to bring out as many supporting documents as he could.

He'd been unable to obtain originals, but he had collected a surprising number of intermediate drafts and working copies. These had been passed around and traded back and forth, like any documents in any bureaucracy, never mind how limited the distribution. As a result, several of them were complete with handwritten marginal notations.

Handwritten by whom?

He recognized Shabnan's handwriting and Ulricka's, and he could only think that the rude masculine scrawls were Narmer's.

The documents themselves made interesting reading, to put it mildly. It was the notations that cinched Jinhai's gut.

He double-sealed his final report in an official clergy-confidential envelope.

Luckily, his handler, Ziellottes, was in Maryhill on unrelated business, so the normal delays would not come into it. Jinhai had no idea what that business might be. Ziellottes was a man of many talents, many interests, and few revelations.

The canons permitted no one to interfere with the delivery of a clergy-confidential envelope and no one other than the envelope's designated recipient to open it.

As a result, even an officer of the guard would think twice about intercepting such a message.

But what about Colonel Chiharu, the guard's commander?

Jinhai tapped the envelope against the palm of his left hand.

Clergy confidentiality offered scant protection from the likes of the good colonel, but it might hold her at bay long enough.

If she had any shred of hard proof, the sort of evidence that would allow her to violate clergy confidentiality, she would have already arrested him. Besides, if she were in fact playing him on a long line, she would let the message go through, hoping to catch his contact at the other end.

Ziellottes would be safe enough. No doubt he, or his agents, had installed numerous cutouts along the way.

Yes, the message would to be safe enough.

Jinhai went down to the rectory office, picked one of the duty couriers at random, handed him the envelope, and sent him on his way.

Goddess bless!

About the Author

Jamie McNabb writes in several genres, but concentrates on science fiction and fantasy. His work appears in the *Universe Between*, *Past Crimes*, *Pulse Pounders*, *Valor*, and other issues of *Fiction River*, as well as in a variety of online and print publications.

Jamie has sailed extensively on the Columbia and Willamette rivers, where *The Assassins of Harmony* series takes place.

For further information and to subscribe to his newsletter, please visit his website: www.jamicmcnabb.com or go to https://landing.mailerlite.com/webforms/landing/w7k8s7.